## "Damn You For This," He Muttered. "You're Not The Only One Who Can't Forget."

Even if she hadn't felt his powerful arousal against her, his blazing eyes betrayed his potent need. Then his gaze hardened with determination, and she watched breathlessly as he lowered his mouth to hers.

"I shouldn't do this," he whispered fiercely, bending her backward, molding her even more tightly to the hard contours of his body. "God help me, I know what you are, what you did."

"You did things too…." He'd hurt her terribly. Yet she wanted him, ached for him.

"But I can't stop myself," he muttered. "But then I never could where you were concerned."

Dear Reader,

When you're an author, occasionally you write a story that grips you more profoundly than some of your others. *A Scandal So Sweet* is such a book.

When I read, I enjoy escaping to worlds of grand passion and enduring romance. Maybe that's why I've written so many stories of reunited lovers.

We all have those people in our lives we never forget. My lovers in *A Scandal So Sweet* have never succeeded in forgetting one another. Torn apart by scandal and betrayal in their youth, they become driven people who are both immensely successful in their careers, but their lives feel incomplete until they meet again.

Their passion reignites in an instant, and despite all the reasons they should remain apart, they find themselves irresistibly attracted to the love that is most dangerous for them.

Ann

# ANN MAJOR

# A SCANDAL SO SWEET

HARLEQUIN®
entertain, enrich, inspire™

Recycling programs
for this product may
not exist in your area.

ISBN-13: 978-0-373-73180-0

A SCANDAL SO SWEET

## Books by Ann Major

**Harlequin Desire**

*Marriage at the Cowboy's Command* #2101
*Terms of Engagement* #2131

**Silhouette Desire**

*Midnight Fantasy* #1304
*Cowboy Fantasy* #1375
*A Cowboy & a Gentleman* #1477
*Shameless* #1513
*The Bride Tamer* #1586
*The Amalfi Bride* #1784
*Sold into Marriage* #1832
*Mistress for a Month* #1869
*\*The Throw-Away Bride* #1912
*\*The Bride Hunter* #1945
*To Tame Her Tycoon Lover* #1984
*Ultimatum: Marriage* #2041

**MIRA Books**

*The Girl with the Golden Spurs*
*The Girl with the Golden Gun*
*The Secret Lives of Doctors' Wives*

\*Golden Spurs

Other titles by this author available in ebook

## *ANN MAJOR*

lives in Texas with her husband of many years and is the mother of three grown children. She has a master's degree from Texas A&M at Kingsville, Texas, and is a former English teacher. She is a founding board member of the Romance Writers of America and a frequent speaker at writers' groups.

Ann loves to write—she considers her ability to do so a gift. Her hobbies include hiking in the mountains, sailing, ocean kayaking, traveling and playing the piano. But most of all, she enjoys her family. Visit her website at www.annmajor.com.

A special thank-you to Stacy Boyd, my editor,
for her patience and brilliance.

A special thank-you to Nicole, a fan who sent me
an email encouraging me while writing this book.

And a thank-you to Ted.

# Prologue

*Houston, Texas*

A man's life could change in a heartbeat.

Seven days ago Zach Torr had been in the Bahamas, elated to be closing the biggest deal of his career. Then he'd received an emergency call about his uncle.

The one person who'd held Zach's back these past fifteen years was gone.

Now, still dressed in the suit he'd worn to give his uncle's eulogy, Zach stood on the same narrow girder from which his uncle had fallen. He stared fearlessly down at his contractors, bulldozers, generators, cranes and men, big tough men, who appeared smaller than ants in their yellow hard hats sixty-five stories below.

Zach was a tall man with thick black hair and wide shoulders; a man his competitors swore was as ruthless as the fiercest jungle predator. The women he'd left behind agreed, saying he'd walked out on them without ever looking back.

Normally, his eyes were colder than black ice. Today they felt moist and stung. How had Uncle Zachery felt when he'd stood here for the last time?

A shudder went through Zach. Men who walked iron were no less afraid of heights than other men.

The chill breeze buffeting him whipped his tie against his face, almost causing him to step backward. He froze, caught his balance…hissed in a breath. A sneeze or a slip— was that how it had happened? Up here the smallest mistake could be fatal.

Had Uncle Zachery jumped? Been startled by a bird? Been pushed? Suffered a heart attack? Or simply fallen as the fore-man had said? Zach would never know for sure.

As Uncle Zachery's sole heir, Zach had endured several tough interviews with the police.

The newspaper coverage had been more critical of him than usual because he'd stayed in the Bahamas to close the deal before coming home.

He hated the invasion of the limelight, hated being writ-ten about by idiots who went for the jugular with or without the facts.

Because the fact was, for Zach, the world had gone dark after that phone call.

When he'd been nineteen and in trouble with the law for something he hadn't done, Uncle Zachery had come back to Louisiana from the Middle East, where he'd been building a city for a sheik. Uncle Zachery had saved him. If not for his uncle, Zach would still be serving hard time.

Houston-bred, Zach had been cast out of town by his beau-tiful stepmother after his father's death. Her reason—she'd wanted everything. His father had naively assumed she'd be generous with his sixteen-year-old son and had left her his entire fortune.

If it hadn't been for Nick Landry, a rough Louisiana shrimper who'd found Zach in a gutter after he'd been beaten by his stepmother's goons, Zach might not have survived. Nick had taken Zach to his shack in Bonne Terre, Louisiana, where Zach had spent three years.

It was in Bonne Terre where he'd met the girl he'd given his heart and soul to. It was in Bonne Terre where he'd been charged with statutory rape. And it was in Bonne Terre where the girl he'd loved had stood silently by while he was tried and condemned.

Fortunately, that's when Uncle Zachery had returned. He'd discovered his sister-in-law's perfidy, tracked Zach to Louisiana, gone up against the town of Bonne Terre and won. He'd brought Zach back to Houston, educated him and put him to work. With his powerful uncle behind him, Zach had become one of the richest men in America.

His cell phone vibrated. He strode off the girder and to the lift, taking the call as he descended.

To his surprise it was Nick Landry.

"Zach, I feel bad about your uncle, yes. I be calling you to offer my condolences. I read about you in the papers. I be as proud as a papa of your accomplishments, yes."

So many people had called this past week, but this call meant everything. For years, Zach had avoided Nick and anything to do with Bonne Terre, Louisiana, but the warmth in Nick's rough voice cheered him.

"It's good to hear from you."

"I've missed you, yes. And maybe you miss me a little, too? I don't go out in the boat so often now. I tell people it be because the fishin' ain't so good like it used to be, but maybe it's just me and my boat, we're gettin' old."

Zach's eyes burned as he remembered the dark brown waters of the bayou and how he'd loved to watch the herons skim low late in the evening as the mist came up from the swamp.

"I've missed you, too, yes," he said softly. "I didn't know how much—until I heard your voice. It takes me back."

Not all his memories of Bonne Terre were bad.

"So why don't you come to Bonne Terre and see this old man before he falls off his shrimp boat and the crabs eat him?"

"I will."

"We'll go shrimpin' just like old times."

After some quick goodbyes, Zach hung up, feeling better than he had in a week.

Maybe it was time to go back to Bonne Terre.

Then he thought about the Louisiana girl he'd once loved— blonde, blue-eyed, beautiful Summer, with the sweet, innocent face and the big dreams. The girl who'd torn out his heart.

She lived in New York now, a Broadway actress. Unlike him, she was the press's darling. Her pictures were everywhere.

Did she ever come home…to Bonne Terre?

Maybe it was time he found out.

# One

*Eight Months Later*
*Bonne Terre, Louisiana*

Zach Torr was back in town, stirring up trouble for her, and because he was, a tumult of dark emotions consumed her.

Summer Wallace parked her rental car in front of Gram's rambling, two-story home. Sighing because she dreaded the thought of tangling with her grandmother and her brother over Zach, she took her time gathering her bag, her purse and her briefcase. Then she saw the loose pages of her script on the floorboard and the slim white Bible she kept with her always. Picking them up, she jammed them into her briefcase.

When she finally slammed the door and headed toward the house she saw Silas, Gram's black-and-white cat, napping in the warm shade beneath the crape myrtle.

"You lazy old thing."

A gentle wind swayed in the dogwood and jasmine, carry-

ing with it the steamy, aromatic scent of the pine forest that
fringed her grandmother's property. Not that Summer was
in the mood to enjoy the lush, verdant, late-August beauty
of her childhood home. No, she was walking through the
sweltering heat toward a sure argument with Gram. About
Zach, of all people.

Fifteen years ago, when she'd run away after her mother's
death, she'd felt sure he was out of her life forever.

Then Gram had called a week ago.

It had been late, and Summer had been dead on her feet
from workshopping an important new play.

"You'll never guess who's making a big splash here in
Bonne Terre, buying up property to develop into a casino,"
Gram had said in a sly tone.

Gram had a habit of calling late and dropping her little
bombs in a seemingly innocent way, so, wary, Summer had
sunk into her favorite chair and curled up to await the ex-
plosion.

"And who do you think bought the old Thibodeaux place
and hired your brother Tuck as his pool boy and all-around
gopher?" her grandmother had asked.

Tuck had a job? This should have been good news. Gram
had been worried about him after his latest run-in with Sheriff Arcenaux. But somehow Summer had known the news
wouldn't be good.

"Okay! *Who?*"

"*Zach* Torr."

Summer had frozen. Her brother, who had poor judgment
in nearly every area of his life, could not work for Zach, who
couldn't possibly have her family's best interests at heart. Not
after what had happened. Not when their names would be forever linked in the eyes of the media and, therefore, the world.

She'd become too famous and he too rich, and their tragic
youthful love affair was too juicy. And every time the story

was rehashed, it always surprised her how much it still hurt, even though she was seen as the innocent victim and he the villain.

From time to time, she'd read about how hard and cold he was now. She'd never forget the story about how ruthlessly he'd taken revenge on his stepmother.

Any new connection between Zach and her family was a disaster in the making.

"You're not the only former resident of Bonne Terre who's famous, you know."

Summer's breath had caught in her throat as she'd struggled to take the news in.

"Zach's a billionaire now."

Summer had already known that, of course. Everybody knew that.

"Even so, he's not too busy to stop by to play Hearts with an old lady when he's in town…or to tell me how Tuck's doing on the job."

Zach had been taking the time to play cards with Gram? To personally report on Tuck, his pool boy? *This was bad.*

"Gram, he's just trying to get to me."

"Maybe this isn't about you. You two were finished fifteen years ago."

Yes, it had been fifteen years. But it *was* about her. She was sure of it.

Summer had tried to make Gram understand why Tuck had to quit his job, but Gram, who'd been exasperated by all the stunts Tuck had pulled ever since high school, had refused to hear anything against Zach, whom she now saw as her knight in shining armor. Then she'd punched Summer's guilt button.

"You never come home, and Zach's visits are fun. He's awful good with Tuck. Why, the other night he and Nick took Tuck shrimping."

"A billionaire in a shrimp boat?"

"Yes, well he did buy Nick a brand-new boat, and his men are remodeling Nick's shack. And you should see Zach. He's lean and fit and more handsome than ever."

*Lean and fit. Rich and handsome.* She'd seen his photos in the press and knew just how handsome he was. Oh, why couldn't he be the no-good homeless person her stepfather had predicted he'd be?

"Rich as he is—an old lady like me with a beautiful, un-married granddaughter can't help wondering why a catch like him is still single."

"Gram! We have a history. An unsavory, scandalous history that I'm sure he wants to forget as much as I do! Not that that's possible when there are always reporters around who love nothing better than to rehash the dirt in celebrities' lives. Don't you see, I can't afford to have anything to do with him."

"No, your stations in life have changed. You're both enor-mously successful. Your career would threaten most men, but it wouldn't threaten Zach. Whatever happened to letting bygones be bygones?"

"Not possible! He hates me!" *And with good reason.*

"Well, he's never said a word about that scandal or against you. You wouldn't be so dead set against him, either—if you saw him. The townspeople have changed their narrow minds about him. Well, everybody except Thurman."

Thurman was Summer's impossible stepfather.

There was no arguing with Gram. So here Summer was— home in Bonne Terre—to remove Tuck from his job and, by doing so, remove Zach from their lives. She didn't want to confront Zach, and maybe, if she could get through to Tuck and Gram, she wouldn't have to. All it had ever taken for Summer to remember the secrets and heartbreak of her past, and the man who'd caused them, was to visit Gram.

Nothing ever changed in Bonne Terre.

Here, under the ancient cypress trees that edged the bayou,

as she listened to a chorus of late-summer cicadas and endured the stifling heat, the wounds to her soul felt as fresh and raw as they had fifteen years ago.

Unlike Tuck, Summer had been an ambitious teen, one who'd decided that if she couldn't have Zach Torr, she had to forget him and follow her dreams. That's what had been best for everybody.

She'd worked hard in her acting career to get where she was, to prove herself. She was independent. Famous, even. And she was happy. Very happy. So happy she'd braved coming back to Bonne Terre for the first time in two years.

Summer pushed the screen door open and let it bang behind her.

"I'm home!"

Upstairs she heard a stampede of footsteps. "Gram, she's here!"

Yanking earbuds from his ears, Tuck slid down the banister with the exuberance of an overgrown kid. She was about to cry out in fear that he'd slam into the newel post and kill himself, but he hopped off in the nick of time, landing on his feet as deftly as a cat.

"Come here and give me a hug, stranger," she whispered.

Looking sheepish, with his long hair falling over his eyes and his baseball cap on backward, Tuck shyly obliged. But then he pulled away quickly.

"If I didn't know better, I'd say you were even taller," she said."

"No, you're shorter."

"Am not!" she cried.

"God, this place is quiet without you here to fight with."

"I do have a career."

"It must be nice," he muttered. "My famous sister."

"I'm doing what I love, and it's great," she said much too

enthusiastically. "Just great. I'm here to try to teach you about ambition."

"I got a job. Didn't Gram tell you?"

Gram walked into the room and took Summer into her arms before Summer could reply.

"I was wondering what it would take to get my Babygirl home."

"Don't you dare call me that!" Summer smiled, fondly remembering how she used to be embarrassed by the nickname when she was a teenager.

"Set your bag down and then go sit out on the screened porch. Tuck, you join her. I'll bring you something you can't get in that big city of yours, Babygirl—a glass of my delicious, mint-flavored tea."

Summer sighed. "Gram, I don't want you wearing yourself out waiting on us. Tuck, we're going to help her, you hear?"

Tuck, who was lazy by nature, frowned, but since he adored his big sister, he didn't argue. He trailed behind them into the kitchen where he leaned against a wall and watched them do everything.

"At least you're going to carry the tray," Summer ordered as she placed the last tea cup on it.

Tuck grabbed a chocolate-chip cookie instead.

Then the phone rang and he shrugged helplessly before disappearing to answer it.

As Summer took the tray out to the porch and set it on the table, she sank into her favorite rocker, finally taking the time to appreciate the deep solitude of the trees that wrapped around Gram's big old house. In New York or L.A., Summer's phones rang constantly with calls from her agent, producers and directors…and, especially of late, reporters.

She was A-list now, sought after by directors on both coasts. She'd worked hard and was living her dream.

She had it all.

Or so she'd believed. Then her costar and sometimes lover, Edward, had walked out on her. The night their hit play closed, he'd declared to the entire cast that he was through with her. That had been a month ago. Ever since, nosy reporters had been hounding her for the full story, which she still didn't want to share. That night, back in her apartment after the wrap party, she'd tried to tell herself that Edward's departure hadn't made her painfully aware of how empty her personal life had become.

No well-known Broadway actress was ever alone, especially when she was under contract for a major Hollywood film. Even when she was between shows and movies, she couldn't walk out of her apartment without some stranger trying to take her picture or get her autograph. She was always multitasking—juggling workshops, PR events, rehearsals and script readings. Who had time for a personal life?

She was thirty-one. Forty, that age that was the death knell to actresses, didn't seem quite so far away anymore. And Gram, being old-fashioned and Southern, constantly reminded Summer about her biological clock. Lately, Gram had started emailing pictures of all Summer's childhood girlfriends' children and gushing about how cute they were.

"Where would I be without you and Tuck? Mark my words, you'll be sorry if you end up old and alone."

Gram's longings were part of the reason Summer had let Hugh Jones, the hottest young actor on the west coast, rush her into a new relationship not two weeks after Edward had jilted her so publicly. Had she actually felt a little desperate at realizing how alone she was?

Not wanting to think about her personal life a moment longer, Summer picked up her glass and drank some of her iced tea.

Where was Gram? And what was taking Tuck so long on the phone?

Was he talking to Zach?

She took another sip of tea.

Reporters constantly asked her if she was in love with Hugh. But unfortunately for her, it wasn't Hugh who came to mind at the mention of the word *love*. No, for her, love and Zach would always be tangled together like an impossible knot. Her chest tightened. She'd only felt that exquisitely painful rush of excitement once.

She never wanted to feel it again.

She'd been sixteen, and he nineteen, when their romance had ended in unbearable heartbreak. For a brief moment she allowed herself to remember New Orleans and the terrible, secret loss she'd suffered there, a loss that had shattered her youthful illusions forever, a loss that had taught her some mistakes could never be made right.

*Zach* was the reason why she almost never came home. Bonne Terre was a small, gossipy Cajun town. If she hadn't forgotten her past, the town wouldn't have forgotten it, either. Even if the town's citizens didn't ask her about him, she always *felt* him everywhere when she was home. She had too many painful memories and…secrets.

Here on this very porch *he* had kissed her that first time.

Just as she was remembering how her mouth had felt scorched after he'd brushed his lips against hers, her grandmother's low, gravelly whisper interrupted her thoughts.

"You're not the only person who loves to sit in that chair."

The sly, mischievous note in her grandmother's tone sent a frisson of alarm through Summer.

"Oh." She didn't turn and smile because her cheeks were still burning.

"Zach always sits there."

Summer stiffened.

"I can't believe you allow him to come over, much less allow him to sit in *my* chair. What if someone tips off the

ANN MAJOR                                          19

press about his visits to see my grandmother and this causes
another nasty story to be published about us? And why is he
developing in Bonne Terre anyway? In all these years he's
never once come back, until now."

"When his uncle died back in the fall he came to visit Nick.
When he saw the land prices, he started talking to people.
He already has a casino in Vegas. One thing led to another.
The city fathers decided to court him…."

When Summer noticed the ice cubes in her glass tinkling,
she set the glass down with a harsh *clink*.

"Careful, dear, that's your mama's best crystal." They
paused, as they both reflected on the sweetness of Anna,
Summer's dear, departed mother, whom they would miss forever. "Zach's bought up all that land across from our place."

"I still can't believe that with his history, with so many
in this town set against him, Zach would come back here."

"He says it's time to set the record straight. He's certainly
winning the town over."

How exactly did he intend to set the record straight? Summer thought of the one secret she'd kept from him and trembled. "He's made a fortune in Houston. Isn't that vindication
enough? Why would he care what the people here think of
him?"

"They nearly sent him to prison."

*Because of me,* Summer thought with genuine regret.

"Old wounds run deep sometimes…and need healin'. He's
got everybody around here excited. His casino's going to be
a fancy riverboat."

"Gambling? It's a vicious, addictive sport."

"Gaming will bring jobs…. And jobs will buy a lot of forgiveness. Bonne Terre's fallen on really hard times of late."

"Gram, you sound brainwashed. It makes me wonder how
often Zach comes by."

"Well, he dropped by the first time because he wanted to see if I'd sell this place to him."

Summer would watch the swamp freeze over before she let that happen.

"Zach's been by about once a week ever since. We have coffee and cookies. Chocolate chip are his favorite."

Summer took great pains to center her glass in its condensation ring on the coaster. "I hope you didn't tell Zach you might sell or that I was coming to see you about all this."

Her grandmother hesitated. "I'm afraid I might have told him he could make me an offer. And… You know how I can never resist bragging about you. I've shown him my scrapbooks."

Summer frowned. "I can't imagine I'm his favorite subject."

"Well, like I said, he's always ever-so polite. He's been especially interested in your romance with Hugh." Gram smiled. "Asked me whom I thought was more fun—Hugh or himself?

I said Hugh was a rich movie star, who probably wouldn't waste his time on an old lady. I told Zach he had nothing to worry about."

Summer squeezed her eyes shut and counted to ten.

Kneading the knot between her eyes, she said, "Did you or didn't you tell him I was coming home because I'm upset about Tuck's job?"

"It's hard for me to remember exactly what I do or say these days, but if I did tell him, what can it matter? You said that what happened between you two was over a long time ago."

Summer frowned. Yes, of course, it was over. So, why was she obsessing about him?

"I think Thurman had Zach all wrong. I told your stepfather he was too hard on the boy at the time, that you were just youngsters in love. But Thurman doesn't ever listen to anybody."

He hadn't listened when Summer and her mother had begged him to drop the charges against Zach, and the stress of that time had ended her mother's remission. Her mother's death was just one of the reasons Summer was estranged from him. The other had to do with a tiny grave in New Orleans.

But Summer didn't want to think about that. "Okay, back to selling this place to Zach. That can't happen."

"I can't help it if I'm not averse to moving into a modern condo, if Zach comes up with some favorable financin'."

"But I love this house," Summer protested. "I can't believe you've actually gone this far with a deal without once mentioning it to me. What's his next move?"

"He said he'd put an offer together, but so far he's been too busy."

"Maybe we'll get lucky and he'll stay busy," Summer muttered, squeezing her eyes shut.

Somehow she didn't really think Zach, who could be relentless, would leave her grandmother alone until he got exactly what he wanted. Had he hired Tuck to win over Gram? So she'd sell him her home, which had been in the family for more than a hundred years?

"Word has it he closed on that tract across from us just yesterday. That's where he'll build the dock," Gram said. "So he'd like to control this property. He definitely doesn't want me selling to anybody else."

Inspiration struck.

"Gram, I'll buy the house from you. Then you can live here or in a condo. Your choice."

"Oh?"

"I want you to call Zach and tell him you won't sell. Hopefully, when he learns I'm here checking up on you, he'll back off."

Her grandmother watched her intently for a long moment. "You never looked at Edward the way you used to look at Zach. Fifteen years is a long time for you to still be bothered by a man," said her grandmother wisely. "Have you ever asked yourself why?"

"No." Summer yanked her scrunchy out of her hair and pulled her ponytail even tighter. "Because I'm perfectly happy with my life as it is. Can we quit talking about him and not start on your dissatisfaction with my single state?"

"Oh, all right, dear. I won't bring him up again—or the fact that you're an old maid—not unless you do."

"Old maid? Gram, there's no such thing anymore."

"Maybe that's so in Manhattan, but that's definitely not so in Bonne Terre. Ask anybody."

Gram's set expression stung way more than it should have.

Tuck stuck his head out the door. "Zach called and needs me to come in, so I've got to get to work."

"Hey, Tuck, your job is one of the reasons I came home. Can we talk?" Summer said.

"Later. He needs me to run an errand."

Summer ground her teeth as she watched her brother lope out the door.

Tuck refused to quit his job. Summer and he had quarreled about it briefly, but Zach had just promoted Tuck to full-time status and he now spent his whole day running errands for Zach's contractor.

As for Gram, she was as good as her word. Two whole days had passed without her ever once mentioning Zach.

She was the only one silent on the subject, however. The whole town was buzzing because Summer and Zach were both in town. Whenever Summer went shopping, the curious sneaked sidelong glances at her. The audacious stopped her on the street and demanded to know how she felt about Zach now.

"Do you regret what you and Thurman did—now that Zach's so rich and nice and set on saving this town from economic disaster?" Sally Carson, the postmistress, had demanded.

"Your grandmother told me he's been real sweet to her, too," Margaret York, one of Gram's oldest friends, said with a look of envy.

"Well, his return to this town has nothing to do with me," Summer replied.

"Doesn't it?" Margaret's face was sly and eager. "Men don't forget...."

"Well, I have."

"I wonder how you'll feel when you see him again. *We all wonder.*"

One of the worst things about fame was that it made everyone think they had a right to know about her private life. Some things were too personal and painful to share with anyone, even well-meaning neighbors.

So Summer stopped going into town. Instead, she stayed at the house to work on her script and formulate a new way to approach Tuck.

On this particular afternoon she'd set a plate of cookies and a glass of tea garnished with a sprig of mint beside a chaise longue on the screened veranda. She paced in frustration, gesturing passionately as she fought to discover her character, a young mother. The role eluded Summer because, for her, young motherhood was a painful theme.

But today she did something she'd never let herself do before—remember how she'd felt in New Orleans when she'd been expecting her own child. Suddenly, she broke through the protective walls inside her, and grief washed over her in waves.

Her eyes grew wet, and she began to tremble, but she didn't relent. So deeply was she immersed in painful memories, she didn't hear the hard, purposeful crunch of gravel beneath a man's boots until he was nearly upon her.

A low vicious oath startled her. Expecting Tuck, Summer whirled, dabbing at her damp eyes with the back of her hand.

And there *he* was.

At the sight of Zach's hard, chiseled features swimming through her tears, the pages she'd been holding fell to the wooden floor.

"Well, hello there," he said.

"Zach." She hated the way his low, velvet voice made her heart accelerate, made the air feel even hotter. Frantically, she dabbed at her eyes so he wouldn't see her tears. "Gram said you'd been visiting a lot." Her voice sounded choked and unnatural.

"Did she?" Black eyes narrowed as he pushed the screen door open. "She told me you were coming home." Zach scowled. "You're pale, and your eyes are red. Have you been crying?"

"No! It's nothing," she whispered. "I was just acting out a part."

His lips thinned. "You always were damn talented at that."

Good, he bought it.

Tall and dark in a long-sleeved white shirt and jeans, and as lethally handsome as ever, Zach's tight expression told her he wasn't happy to see her.

As she bent over to retrieve her script, his insolent dark eyes raked her body in a way that made her aware of how skimpily clad she was in her snug blue shorts and thin, clingy blouse.

Feeling strangely warm and too vulnerable suddenly, she bristled and sprang to her feet. "I told Gram to tell you. If she decides to sell, she'll sell to me. So, why are you here now?"

"I haven't spoken to her. My secretary arranged my appointment with your grandmother," he said, striding closer. "When I saw you in those shorts, I imagined she told you I was coming and you were lying in wait...."

"As if I'd do—and, hey, it's August. I...I have a perfect right to wear shorts," she sputtered.

"Yes." His gaze drifted over her appreciatively. "You look good in them. Too good—which I'm sure you know."

"Gram didn't tell me you were coming."

"And she didn't tell me to cancel my visit. I wonder why. Maybe she likes my company. Or maybe she'd prefer to sell to me. This old place and that brother of yours are way too much for her."

"None of that is any of your business."

"Your Tuck was running pretty wild, got himself fired from a bar because money went missing...."

"As if you know anything about Tuck. He doesn't steal!"

Zach's black brows arched. "Still thinking the worst of me while you defend everybody else. Your stepfather's been giving me hell, too."

The comparison to her stepfather cut her...deeply. Zach hadn't been there for her when she'd needed him either, had he? He hadn't cared....

*Maybe because he hadn't known.*

"As a matter of fact, I like your grandmother. That's why I hired Tuck. When I happened on him late one night, he'd had a flat tire. He didn't have a spare or money or a credit card, and his phone was dead. So he accepted my offer to haul him to a service station and buy him a new tire on the condition that he become my pool and errand boy and work it off."

"I see through your Good Samaritan act."

"I was sort of suspicious about it myself."

"You're just using Tuck to get at me in some way. So go,"

she whispered. "You are the last person I want involved with my family, especially with Tuck, who's extremely vulnerable."

"Well, sorry if my return to Bonne Terre upsets you, or if Tuck's being my employee bothers you," he said, not sounding the least apologetic. "But since I've got business in this town for some time to come, and Tuck works for me, I suppose you and I were bound to meet again...sooner or later."

"Gambling? Is that your business?"

"Yes. What of it? You're an actress, someone skilled at weaving seductive illusions. You sure seduced me with your little act. And I let you off easy. You should feel lucky. I'm not known for lenience with people who betray me."

Easy? Lucky? New Orleans lay like a weight on her heart.

"All you see is your side."

"I was the one who damn near got strung up because of your lies," he said. "I'm the one who's still found guilty every time some reporter decides to write another story about us."

"Well, maybe you don't know everything!" She stopped. She would never make the mistake of trying to confide in him. But despite her best intentions, she said, "You...you can't believe I ever wanted to accuse you, not when I begged you to run off with me, and when it was my idea to..."

"To seduce me?" he finished.

His silky whisper and the intense fire in his black eyes rubbed her nerves raw.

"It wasn't like that and you know it. I...I couldn't help it if Thurman hated you for what I did."

"Let's not kid ourselves. You did what you did. I don't give a damn anymore about why you did it."

Shame and some darker emotion she didn't want him to sense scorched her cheeks as she turned away from the coldness in his face. "If I could have undone what I did or said, or what I caused people to believe about you, I would have."

"Hollow words...since you could have stepped up and

cleared my name at any point. You didn't. Like a fool, I waited for you to do just that. I was young. I believed in you back then." His mouth tightened into a hard, forbidding line. "But, no, you ran off to New Orleans where you probably seduced somebody else."

"There was never anyone but you…." She swallowed tightly. "I—I tried to apologize…and explain. You refused to take my calls. I even went to Houston looking for you after your uncle took you away, but you wouldn't see me."

"By then I knew what a talented manipulator you were."

At his dark, unforgiving scowl, she sucked in a tortured breath. "If you hate me so much, why won't you just go?"

"I don't hate you. Frankly, I don't consider you worth the waste of any more emotion. What I'm doing here isn't about you. I've made a name for myself in other places. When Nick called me a few months ago, I realized I'd never let go of what happened here and neither have the people of this town or the media. Maybe I've decided it's time I changed a few people's minds.

"Your stepfather used to be the biggest man in these parts. Not anymore. I intend to be bigger than he ever was. I intend to make him pay for what he did—to kill him with kindness, bestowed upon his town."

"I want you to leave Gram and Tuck alone. I'm buying this property from her because I won't have you cheating her to get back at me."

"You'd better not make accusations like that in public."

"And you'd better stop trying to make me look bad to my grandmother, who's started nagging me about not coming home often enough!"

"Haven't you been neglecting her?"

"Well, if I don't come home, it's because of you. I—I can't forget…when I'm home," she finished raggedly.

Dark hurt flashed in his eyes but was gone so fast she was sure she'd only imagined it.

When he stomped toward the front door, she blocked his way. At her nearness, his hard body tensed. When their gazes locked, a muscle in his jawline jerked savagely. His breathing had roughened.

He wasn't nearly as indifferent as he'd said.

Nor was she.

"Move aside," he muttered.

Hurt, she lashed out. "No—this is my grandmother's house. I won't allow you to use her to get at me. So—leave."

"Like hell!"

When she stood her ground, his hands closed over her forearms. But as he tried to edge her aside, she stomped down on his foot with her heel.

Cursing, he tightened his grip and crushed her against his muscular length.

Despite the unwanted shiver of excitement his touch caused, her tone was mild. "Would you please let me go?"

A dozen warring emotions played across his dark face as she struggled to free herself.

"I don't think I will."

Locking her slim, wriggling body to his made their embrace even more alarmingly intimate.

"You're trembling," he said. "Why? Are you acting now? Or do you feel what I…." He broke off with a look of self-contempt.

"Damn you for this," he muttered. "You're not the only one who can't forget."

Even if she hadn't felt his powerful arousal against her pelvis, his blazing eyes betrayed his potent male need. Then his gaze hardened with determination, and she watched breathlessly as he lowered his mouth to hers.

"I shouldn't do this," he whispered fiercely, bending her

backward, molding her even more tightly to the hard contours of his body. "God help me, I know what you are, what you did."

"You did things, too...." He'd hurt her terribly. Yet she wanted him, ached for him.

"I can't stop myself," he muttered. "But then I never could where you were concerned."

No sooner did his warm mouth close over hers than she turned to flame. If he'd flung her onto the chaise longue and followed her down, she would have forgotten the hurt that had turned her heart to stone for fifteen years. She would have ripped his jeans apart at the waist, sliding her hands inside.

She wanted to touch him, kiss him everywhere, wind her legs and arms around him and surrender completely—even though she knew his need was based on the desire to punish while hers was due to temporary insanity.

On a sigh, her arms circled his tanned neck, and she clung, welding herself to his lean frame in a way that told him all that she felt. She was a woman now, a woman whose needs had been too long denied. When he shuddered violently, she gasped his name.

"Zach... I'm sorry," she murmured as warm tears leaked from her eyes and trickled down her cheek. She feathered gentle fingertips through his thick, inky hair. "I wronged you, and I'm so sorry. For years I've wanted to make it up to you." She hesitated. "But... You hurt me, too."

For fifteen years, she'd been dead in the arms of every other man who'd held her.

She hadn't felt this alive since she'd last been in Zach's embrace.

His hand closed over her breast, stroking a nipple until it hardened. The other hand had moved down to cup her hip.

Next he undid the buttons of her blouse so that it parted for his exploration. For one glorious moment she was her younger self and wildly in love with him again. Back then she had trusted him completely. She'd given him everything of herself. With a sigh, she leaned into him as he stroked her, and her response sent him over some edge.

He rasped in a breath. Then, in the next shuddering instant, he ended their kiss, tearing his lips free, leaving her desolate, abandoned.

Loosening his grip, he let her go and staggered free of her as if he'd been burned. He raked a large, shaking hand through his hair and swore violently, staring anywhere but at her.

"Damn you," he muttered, inhaling deeply. "I see why you do so well on Broadway. You're like a tigress in heat. Is that why Hugh Jones took up with you so fast?"

Summer was about to confess she felt nothing when Hugh kissed her—nothing—but Zach spoke first.

"Brilliant performance," he said. "You deserve an Oscar."

"So do you," she whispered in breathless agony as she dried her cheeks with the back of her hand. She couldn't let him know that for a few magical seconds she'd actually cared.

"I'd better go before I do something incredibly stupid," he said.

"Like what?" she murmured, feeling dazed from his mesmerizing kiss and savage embrace.

"Like take you back to my house to do whatever the hell I want to do with you…for as long as I want."

"Oh?"

"Don't look at me like that! I know what you are. Damn you for making me want the impossible," he muttered.

She clenched her fists, not any happier than he was to realize that she wanted the impossible, too.

He didn't like her. With good reason. Their past was too painful to revisit. What burned inside her, and in him, was lust—visceral and destructive.

Gram opened the front door. Her violet, silver-lashed eyes wide, she peered out at them with excessive interest, causing Summer, whose blouse was still unbuttoned, to blush with shame even as she quickly pulled the edges back together. The last thing she wanted to do was get Gram's hopes up about a romantic reunion with Zach.

"Oh, my go-o-o-d-ness." Gram worked hard to hide her pleasure at the sight of Zach's blazing eyes and her granddaughter's scarlet face and state of dishabille. "I'm so sorry." In a softer voice directed toward Summer, she said, "And I thought you told me you wanted nothing more to do with him." There was that sly note of satisfaction in her tone again.

"I don't," Summer cried, but the door had already closed behind her triumphant grandmother. "Why didn't you tell me he was coming over?" she called after Gram. Then Summer turned and said to Zach, "Why did I even ask, when I specifically ordered her not to mention you?"

Zach's eyes went flat and cold. "As far as I'm concerned, this never happened. But—if you see me again—you'd better run. You and I have more unfinished business than I realized. Don't give me any more reasons to come after you and finish what you started."

Suspecting he must want revenge, she swallowed. "Don't threaten me."

"It's not a threat. It's a promise, a warning. If you're smart, you'll stay away from me."

As if to emphasize his words, he strode over to her. Reaching up his hand, he ran a calloused fingertip along her damp cheek, causing her to shiver involuntarily.

"I want you in my bed. I want you to pay for what you did. In every way that I demand."

Startled, because the image he painted—of lying under him on a soft bed—aroused her to such a shocking degree, she jumped back. Out of his sensually lethal reach, her voice was firm. "I won't be seeing you again."

"Good. Tell your grandmother I'll call her after you leave town."

His gorgeous mouth curled. Looking every bit as furious and ashamed as Summer was beginning to feel, Zach turned on his heel and strode down the gravel drive, leaving her to wonder how she could have stood there like a besotted idiot and let him touch her again after sharing such an embarrassing kiss.

"None of this happened," Summer whispered consolingly to herself when she finally heard the roar of his car. Too aware of gravel spinning viciously, she sank down onto the steps and hugged her knees tightly.

She felt cold and hot at the same time.

It was all a horrible mistake. Zach didn't like that it had happened any more than she did.

She was glad he felt that way.

*She was glad!*

Somehow she had to make Gram and Tuck understand that Zach was dangerous, that he'd threatened her.

Tuck, who'd gotten in trouble too many times to count, could not continue to work for Zach, who would use whatever her brother did to his own advantage.

Squaring her shoulders, Summer got to her feet and picked up the remaining pages of her script. Then she ran into the house and up the stairs where she took a long, cold shower and brushed her teeth.

Not that she could wash away his taste or the memory of his touch or the answering excitement in her system.

That night, when she awoke, breathing hard from a vivid dream about Zach kissing her even more boldly, it was impossible to ignore the hunger that was both ancient and familiar lighting every nerve ending in her being.

Wild for him, she sat up in the darkness and pushed her damp hair back from her hot face. "It was just a stupid kiss. It doesn't matter! Zach can't stand me any more than I can stand him."

*So, why are you dreaming about him, aching for him, even when you know he despises you?*

# Two

*One month later*

Once back in New York, Zach's kiss lingered on the edges of Summer's consciousness almost all the time, despite the fact that she'd willed herself to forget him. Despite the fact that she'd decided it was best not to obsess over things she couldn't control, like Tuck's refusal to quit his job and Gram's support of his decision.

And because the memory of Zach's kiss lingered, she drove herself to work harder than ever.

Summer read every script her agent gave her. She auditioned tirelessly for any part that was halfway right for her. When she was home alone she compulsively cleaned and dusted every item in her already immaculate apartment in a vain attempt to shove Zach Torr and his stupid kiss and his ridiculous threats back into the past where they belonged.

Not that she could stop herself from calling certain gossips in Bonne Terre to get a picture of what he was up to back home or stop herself from reading her hometown's newspaper online to get the latest news about his riverboat gambling project. Everything she read was annoyingly favorable. People were more impressed by him every day. He was the town's favorite son. Rumors abounded about the lavishness of the riverboat he was building and the luxurious amenities and hotels he was constructing onshore.

On impulse, maybe to prove to those blockheads back home how little she cared for Zach, she let Hugh Jones join one of her interviews.

Naturally, the young, bright-eyed journalist went gaga over beautiful, golden Hugh, whose immense ego was hugely gratified at being fawned over.

At first, the young woman's eager questions had been standard fare. Summer tossed off her ritual answers.

Her favorite role was the one she was creating. She was always nervous opening nights. And, yes, the play she was workshopping today was ever-so exciting.

Naturally, when the journalist wasn't entirely focused on Hugh, he grew bored.

Hugh shuffled from one foot to the other and yawned, and the reporter laughed and leaned into him so her breast brushed his elbow.

"Okay, let's talk about this hot new man in your life. Every woman in America is dying to be you, Summer." The woman was staring into Hugh's baby-blues as if she'd been hypnotized.

Idiotically, the phrase *hot new man* put Summer back on Gram's screened porch, in the arms of that certain individual she would give anything to forget.

Again she tasted the sweet, blistering warmth of Zach's mouth and felt his muscular length pressing her close. At the memory of his big hands closing over her breast and butt, the dark, musty corner she shared with Hugh and the reporter felt airless.

"So, what's the latest with you and Hugh?" the reporter asked. "If you don't mind my saying so, you two are *the* most exciting couple these days."

"I'm a pretty lucky guy." Hugh squeezed Summer closer before launching into a monologue about himself.

Summer was wondering if she and Hugh had ever once had a real conversation about anything else.

"I don't think Summer's got any complaints," the reporter said when Hugh finally ended the everybody-loves-me monologue.

Hugh laughed, pulled Summer closer and planted his mouth on hers just as a flash blinded her.

Infuriated at his brashness, Summer thumped her fists on his chest. Luckily, her cell phone vibrated and blasted rap music from her pocket.

"Excuse me," she whispered, desperate for an excuse to be done with the reporter and Hugh.

Sliding her phone open, she read the name, *Viola Guidry.* "Sorry, guys, it's my grandmother. I have to take this."

"So—that kiss makes me wonder how serious you and Hugh are?" the reporter asked.

"We're just good friends," Summer snapped in a flat, cool tone.

"That's all you're going to give me—"

Nodding, Summer smiled brightly as she shook the woman's hand. "Thanks so much." Cupping the phone to her ear, Summer walked away.

"Hey, girls, much as I loved doing this interview, I've got a meeting before I catch my plane to L.A.," Hugh said carelessly, blowing Summer an air kiss. "See you, angel."

Summer waved absently and fought to concentrate on her grandmother's frantic words.

"You have to come home! Tuck's in the hospital. He's going to be okay, but Sheriff Arcenaux says he may have to arrest him!"

"For what?"

"Tuck invited some friends over to Zach's and they got into his liquor. When Zach came home, Tuck was so drunk he'd passed out. Two of Zach's cars were missing, and Tuck's friends were busily looting the place."

"Oh, my God! Did I warn you or not?"

"Zach's threatening to press charges. So—you've got to come home."

Fear was a cold fist squeezing Summer's heart so tightly she could barely breathe. Practically speaking, she didn't have time for this. Her calendar was jam-packed with work commitments. Emotionally, she knew her family needed her.

"Zach wants to meet with you. He gave me his attorney's number and told me to have you call him. He said maybe he'd be willing to work something out with you, instead of pressing charges, if you meet with him. But he'll only meet with you."

Summer felt so frustrated and panic-stricken it was all she could do not to throw the phone.

Zach had her right where he wanted her—cornered.

In a soft voice, she said, "I'm on my way, Gram."


She was late.

Zach hated wasting time, and that was exactly what he was doing as he waited for Summer, a woman he'd spent years trying to forget. His empire should be his focus, not some woman from his past.

Hell, he'd wasted too much time worrying about her ever since he'd seen her on Viola's porch. She'd looked so sad and fragile before they'd spoken. He was almost sure she'd been crying. The pain in her eyes had been so profound he still wanted to know what she'd been thinking.

Then, like a fool, he'd kissed her.

Her mouth had been hot and yielding, almost desperate with pent-up passion. But tender, too. Ever since that kiss, it was as if her lips and her taste and her softness and her sweet vulnerability had relit the passion he'd once felt for her. It seemed nothing, not all the ugliness or news coverage or even reason, had been able to destroy his desire for her.

The woman's kiss had made him remember the girl he'd loved and trusted.

She didn't matter; she couldn't ever matter again.

Summer had been a virgin when she'd given herself to him. His one and only. Never would he forget how lush, lovely and shyly innocent she'd been, nor how her shy blue eyes had shone. He'd been deeply touched that such a beautiful girl with such a radiant soul had chosen him.

For the first two years they'd known each other, his focus had been their friendship and protecting her from her controlling stepfather. Then they'd fallen in love during her senior year, so he'd stayed in Bonne Terre to wait for her to graduate. He hadn't pushed for sex, but somehow, after they'd run away together, she'd gotten through his defenses.

One night when they'd been alone in that remote cabin, she'd cried, asking him what she should do about her stepfather. What would happen if they didn't go back, if she didn't finish school? Would he come to New York with her?

He'd realized then that Summer saw him as part of her future; saw her stepfather and Bonne Terre as something she was finished with forever.

Intending to comfort her, to reassure her that he wanted her in his future as well, he'd gone to the bed, taken her in his arms and held her close. Her hair had smelled of jasmine, so he'd nuzzled it. Then she'd kissed him, her soft mouth open, her body pressing against his eagerly. She probably hadn't understood how she'd tempted him.

He'd stroked her hair, caressing her, and she'd moaned.
Her tears had stopped, but she'd clung anyway. Then they'd
come together as if it were the most natural thing in the world.
Their union had been both sexual and spiritual. He'd believed they'd marry after she graduated, that they would be
together forever.

Never again had he felt like that about a woman.

*Forget it.*

Zach forced his mind to the present. He couldn't afford to
reminisce. Time was more precious than money. His uncle's
death had taught him that.

Zach had his briefcase stuffed with foreclosure cases
he'd intended to review as he sat in his attorney's sumptuous
conference room. Waiting for *her*. Plate-glass windows af-
forded him an excellent view of the bayou four stories below.
Not that he was enjoying the scene of cypress and dogwood
trees. No, he couldn't stop thinking about her.

Why was she late? Was she remembering their last en-
counter and his promise to make her pay?

When he heard the desperate click of her high heels in the
hall, he glanced up, tense with expectation. Even as he steeled
himself to feel nothing, his heart began to race.

The door opened, framing her slim, elegant body before
she entered. Her delicate, classical features and radiant com-
plexion were too lovely for words.

He wanted her so much he couldn't breathe.

They looked at each other and then away while the silent
tension between them crackled. On some deep level, she drew
him. Her incredible blond beauty alone made her unforget-
table. Then there was her fame. Hell, how could he forget her
when her face was plastered on the covers of gossip maga-
zines and cheap, weekly newspapers?

*She was everywhere.*

Only a few days ago he hadn't been able to resist reading

the latest about her budding romance with Hugh Jones in one of those sensational newspapers he despised. He'd grabbed it off a wire shelf in a drugstore and jammed it into his briefcase. He'd carried it up to his office and pored over the story that went with the front-page photo of the famous couple sharing a kiss. Summer had claimed they were just friends, but Jones had expounded about how crazy they were about each other. Which one of them was lying?

*Probably her.*

Zach had wadded the newspaper and thrown it in the trash. In his penthouse suite, staring out at the city of Houston, which was littered with the skyscrapers he'd built and owned, he'd never felt more isolated.

She had a life—perhaps she even loved that famous, egotistical movie star—while he had only his fierce ambition and immense wealth. He'd gone through his contact list on his smart phone, called a beautiful blonde who resembled Summer and asked her out. But that night, after dinner, when she'd invited him up to her loft, he'd said he had to work. Driving home, feeling empty and more alone than ever, he'd burned for Summer.

So, he'd seized his opportunity. He'd used her brother to get her here.

"Coffee?" His attorney's pretty secretary offered from the doorway.

"No," Zach thundered without even bothering to ask Summer, for whom he felt irrational fury because she wouldn't stop consuming his thoughts.

He wasn't in the mood for niceties. When the secretary left and Summer's long-lashed, legendary violet-blue eyes flicked in alarm, he felt as if she'd sucker punched him in the gut. Damn her, for having this much power over him.

His heart hardened against her knockout beauty even as other parts of his body hardened because of it. He wished he could forget the softness of her breast and the firmness of her butt and the sweet taste of her lips. He wished he didn't ache to hold her and touch her again. He wanted to kiss her and force her to forget all about Jones.

How many others had there been in her bed since Zach? Legions, he imagined with a rush of bitterness. A Broadway star with a face and figure like hers, not to mention a budding movie career, could have anybody—directors, producers, actors, fans.

Hell, she had Hugh Jones, didn't she? But was she as responsive when Jones touched her? Had Zach only imagined she'd been pushing against Jones, trying to free herself, when that picture had been taken?

None of it mattered. Zach wanted her in his bed with an all-consuming hunger. And he was determined to have her.

As if she read his thoughts, she flushed and glanced down, staring at her white, ice-pick heels rather than at him. Still, her sultry voice made him burn when she whispered, almost shyly, "Sorry I'm late. Traffic. I had to go by Gram's first… to check on Tuck."

"How's he doing?" Zach asked, standing up and placing his hand on the back of the chair he intended to offer her.

He'd found Tuck drunk and unconscious on the living-room floor of Zach's new house. The garage doors had been open, and Zach's Lamborghini and second Mercedes had been missing.

Fortunately, Zach had come home unexpectedly and had caught two of Tuck's friends, also drunk, ransacking his house, or he might have suffered worse losses. Since then, the automobiles had been found abandoned in New Orleans.

Zach blamed himself, in part, for not having hired an appropriate staff for the house.

"Tuck's doing okay." Summer answered his question as she stepped farther into the room, her legs as light and graceful as a dancer's, her silky white dress flowing against her hips. He remembered how sexy she'd looked when she'd bent over in her short shorts on her grandmother's porch.

And why shouldn't she be graceful and sexy? She was a performer, a highly paid one. Everything she did was part of a deliberate, well-rehearsed act. Maybe the kiss they'd shared when she'd seemed to quiver so breathlessly had been a performance, as well.

She sat down in the chair he'd indicated and crossed her legs prettily. He stayed on his feet because staring down at her gave him the advantage.

Even though he knew what she was, and what she was capable of, the years slid away. Again he was sixteen, the bad new homeless kid in school with the sullen, bruised face. Everybody had been scared of him. Summer had been the popular, pampered high-school freshman, a princess who'd had every reason to feel superior to him.

People talked in a town the size of Bonne Terre. Everybody knew everybody. Nobody approved of Nick dragging such a rough kid home and foisting him upon the school. Thurman Wallace had even demanded Zach be thrown out.

Only Summer, who'd been a precocious thirteen and two years ahead of her age in school, hadn't looked down on Zach. Not even when all the other kids and her step-daddy thought she should. No, even on that first day, when Roger Nelson, a football star, had demanded to know what Zach had done to make a guy hate him so much he'd beaten him nearly to death, she'd butted in and defended him.

"Maybe that's not what happened," she'd said. "Maybe Zach was in the right, defending himself, and the other guy was in the wrong. We don't know."

"So what happened, Torr?" Nelson had demanded.

"Why should I tell you?"

"See, he's trash, Pollyanna," Nelson had jeered. "Anybody can see that!"

"Well, then maybe I'm blind, because I can't," she'd insisted. "I see a person who needs a friend."

Not long after that Summer had become his secret best friend.

The memories slipped away, and Zach was heatedly aware of the woman seated before him.

As if she couldn't resist using her power on him, Summer tipped her head his way, sending that thick curtain of blond hair over her shoulders as her blue eyes burned into the center of his soul.

"Zach, thanks for getting Tuck medical attention so fast. They said you had specialists flown in from Houston." Her face was soft, beguilingly grateful.

Clenching a fist, he jammed it in a pocket. He wasn't buying into her gratitude. Not when he knew she'd do anything to keep her brother from being arrested.

"The doctors are personal friends of mine in Houston. It was either fly them here or airlift him to New Orleans. He was out cold. He had a bump the size of a hen's egg on his head and a gash that needed stitches, so I wanted to make sure he was just drunk and that there was no serious head injury involved."

"Thank you," she said.

"I don't see any need for us to make a big deal about something anyone would have done."

"You paid for everything, too. We have insurance. If you'll invoice me, I'll—"

"You'll pay me. Fine," he growled.

He was blown away by his feelings. He wanted her so badly he could think of nothing else, and she was coldly talking money.

"You said you wanted to see me. I've talked to Tuck, and

he feels terrible about everything that happened. He had no idea those boys were going to steal anything or tear up your house. The last thing he remembers is hearing a noise in the garage and stumbling across the living room to check it out. Then he must have tripped."

"Oh, really? What about the money that went missing when he was fired from his last job? Your brother's been running pretty wild all summer. He's nineteen. Old enough to know what the guys he runs around with are capable of."

"He was just showing off. They said they'd never seen a billionaire's place. He wanted to impress them."

"He shouldn't have invited them over or given them my whiskey."

"I agree, and so does he…now. He just didn't think."

"Your Tuck's had too many run-ins with the law for me to buy into his innocence. He's been indulged in Bonne Terre. Maybe because he's a Wallace."

"That's what this is about, isn't it—his last name? You were hoping something like this would happen. You delib- erately hired my trouble-prone brother, set him up, so you could get back at me."

He tensed at her accusation. "Since you're so quick to blame others for his actions, I'm beginning to see why he's so irresponsible."

Heat flared in her eyes. He noted that she was breathing irregularly, that her breasts were trembling.

"You have no right to use him this way. He's practically an orphan. I was twelve when he was born. He was two when our father ran off, four when Mother married Thurman and he adopted us. If my stepfather was hard on me by pushing me in school, demanding I excel and graduate two years ahead of my class, he constantly browbeat Tuck, calling him a wimp and a sissy who'd never amount to anything. I was the favorite. Tuck could never measure up.

"After our mother died, he was raised by a stepfather who disliked him and then by aunts who cared more for their own children, and later by his grandmother, who's become too old and lenient. And I admit, I don't come home often enough."

Zach had figured all that out for himself. The kid had no direction. She and Viola were protective of Tuck, but didn't demand enough responsibility from the boy.

"And what do you do—you put him in temptation's way so you can get at me," she repeated in a shaky tone. "Since he's been in trouble before, if you press charges and he's tried and convicted, he could be locked up for a long time. You knew that when you hired him. If this gets out to the media, there will be a frenzy."

Zach paced to the window. "If you believe I deliberately used Tuck to hurt you, you wouldn't believe anything I told you to defend myself. So, I won't bother."

"Oh, please. You threatened me the last time I saw you. I think you've ordered me here because you intend to make good on that threat!"

*Yes,* he wanted to yell.

*I want to sleep with you so badly I'd do almost anything to accomplish that!*

But then the intensity of her pleading look made him jerk his gaze from hers.

She was afraid of him.

He didn't want her fear. He wanted her warm and passionate and wild, as she'd been the first time.

He strode back to the table and picked up the legal documents in which he'd accused her younger brother of a felony.

When he saw his grip on the papers made his tendons stand out, Zach knew he was dangerously close to losing control. What was her hold over him?

By all rights he should have the upper hand in this situation. Her brother had brought thugs to his home to rip him off. He had every right to demand justice. But Tuck, who'd trusted him, needed help. He needed direction. Zach remembered how he himself had been derailed as a kid due to vengeful adult agendas.

Feeling torn between his ruthless desire and his personal code of ethics, Zach threw the documents onto the table. Then he glared at Summer fiercely, willing revulsion into his gaze.

But she was wide-eyed, vulnerable. Her perfect face was tight-lipped and pale; her shoulders slumped. She'd said she never wanted to see him again, but she'd come today. With a career like hers, she'd probably been busy as hell, but she'd come because she was genuinely worried about her brother and wanted to help him.

When she'd thanked Zach for getting the right doctors, he'd seen real gratitude in her eyes. And he'd liked pleasing her. Too much. In that white dress, which clung in all the right places, she looked young and innocent—not to mention breathtakingly sexy.

He wanted her in his bed. He wanted revenge for all that she'd done to him.

*Do what she's accused you of. Use Tuck. Make your demands.*

Yet something held him back.

For years, he'd told himself he hated her, had willed himself to hate her. But when he'd held her and kissed her at her grandmother's house, his hate had been tempered by softer, more dangerous emotions.

He'd once believed that if he had enough money and power, he would never be vulnerable to the pull of love again.

But now here she was, with her golden hair smelling of perfume and shimmering with coppery highlights so bright they dazzled him, with her lips full and moist, with her long-lashed eyes smoldering with repressed need.

Was she lonely, too? He wanted to hold her against his body and find out.

But more than that, fool that he was, he wanted to protect her. And her idiot brother.

He had to get out of here, go somewhere where he could think this through.

To her, he snarled, "This meeting's canceled." Then he punched the intercom and spoke to his lawyer's secretary. "Tell Davis to take over."

"I don't understand," Summer whispered. "What about Tuck?"

"I'll deal with you two later."

She let out a frightened sigh that cut him to the quick. "Zach, please..."

He wanted to turn to make sure she was all right.

Instead, he shrugged his broad shoulders and sucked in a breath.

To hell with her.

Without a backward glance, he strode out of the room.

# Three

*He was impossible! Arrogant! Rude!*

If he'd slapped her, Zach couldn't have hurt Summer more than he had when he'd turned his back on her and walked out.

Fisting her hands, she got up and ran after him. But with his long legs, the elevator doors were closing before she caught up to him.

"Zach, you've got to listen—"

His glare was indifferent and cold as the doors slammed together.

"Well, you've sure got him on the run. You must have scared the hell out of him," Davis said, chuckling behind her. "That's not so easy to do. Usually he shreds his adversaries."

Zach's attorney looked slim and handsome in his tailored Italian suit and prematurely gray hair. He had been a year or two older than she in high school, but she and he had never been close. Davis worked for Zach now, not her.

Her heart swelled with uncertainty. She was afraid to say

anything to Davis because whatever she said would be repeated to Zach. She couldn't risk damaging Tuck's chances.

"Where do you think he went?" she asked.

"We've got a lot of legal work to wrap up, so he's in town for a few days. He spent his morning at the construction site, and he didn't mention having any other meetings this afternoon, so maybe he went home. I'd leave him alone for now, let him settle down. Don't push him into making a rash decision about Tuck. Believe me, he'll call you when he's ready."

*But wouldn't it be better to deal with him now, when he wasn't ready? Wouldn't that give her an advantage?*

Besides she was under contract to perform in New York, and her calendar was full. She didn't have a second to waste. No way could she stay here indefinitely without major consequences to her career. Directors, producers and other actors were depending on her.

Acting on a mixture of intuition and desperation, she went out to her rental car and followed the winding bayou road to the old Thibodeaux place.

His pale, beige antebellum-style home had a wide front veranda and ten stately columns. Weeds grew in the flower beds, and the grass was overgrown. Wild passion flowers had taken over the edges of the yard. She rang the bell and nobody answered, making her wonder why he didn't have adequate staff.

When she began to pace the veranda, she saw it had a few rotten boards and was in need of a thorough sweeping. She peered through the smudged pane of a front window. Inside, she saw stacks of boxes on the dusty, scarred floors of the palatial rooms.

Apparently, his people hadn't finished moving him in. Was he even here?

When she rang the bell again with no answer, she decided to walk around back by way of a redbrick path that lay in the shade of vast oak trees that needed a good trimming. All the forest-green shutters were peeling, as well.

The mansion had been built a decade before the Civil War and had served as a Yankee headquarters.

Now, the house and yard needed love and lots of money, but with enough of both, it could be a beautiful home for some lucky family. Had Zach bought it because he was thinking of settling down? Marrying and having children? Little dark-haired boys or girls? She imagined them playing out in the yard and hated the way the vision tugged at her heart.

A gleaming silver Mercedes was parked in front of Zach's three-car garage. His car? How many did the man own?

Seeing the low, white-picket fence, also in need of fresh paint, encircling the pool, she opened the gate and stepped gingerly through the high weeds to let herself inside.

Intending to knock on one of the back doors, she headed toward them only to stop when she saw a half-empty bottle of expensive scotch on a nearby table. At the sound of someone bouncing with a vengeance on the diving board, she turned just as a pair of long, tanned, muscular legs disappeared into the water.

"Zach?"

He didn't answer, of course, because he was underwater and speeding like a dark torpedo toward the shallow end. When she heard more splashing, she walked to the edge where the water lapped against the stairs. Centering her white heels precisely on one of the large navy tiles that bordered the pool, she waited for him to come up for air.

He was fast. Obviously, he'd stayed in shape since he'd been on the swim team in high school.

*Oh, my God. He was naked!*

Suppressing a cry at that realization, she saw his clothes discarded untidily on the far side of the pool. Still, instead of turning and fleeing, she stopped and stood her ground.

Her nervous state was such that she felt it took him forever to surface.

Thankfully, since he was in the water, when he did stand up, she couldn't see much of his lower body, but his perfect, muscular, wetly gleaming, tanned torso stimulated her overactive imagination anyway.

He shook his wet black head, flinging droplets of water all over her.

"Hey!" she cried, stepping even farther back.

He scowled up at her in shock even as his black eyes greedily raked her with male interest. Grinning, he made no effort to sink lower in the water or cover himself. "Why am I even surprised?"

"I knocked," she said defensively as hot color rose in her cheeks. "On your front door."

"Did you really?"

A warm breeze caressed her cheek. She looked anywhere except at his wide, dark chest and muscular arms. Even so, she was aware of his height, of his taut stomach and of that dark strip of hair running down his middle and disappearing into the water.

"You didn't answer," she said.

"A lot of women…women who weren't looking for trouble…would have just left."

"I…I'm not looking for trouble."

"Well, you damn sure found it."

"I have to know what you're going to do about Tuck."

"Since you're obviously determined we're going to have a chat on that subject, maybe you'd be so kind as to get me a towel out of the bathhouse. Since I thought I was alone, I didn't think I'd need one. Or… Do I—need one?"

"Yes!" she cried. "You most certainly do!"

He laughed.

Thankful for something to do other than trying to avoid

looking at his amused and much-too-sexy face, she all but flew to the bathhouse. Returning quickly, she set the fluffy, folded rectangle on the edge of the pool. Patting it primly, she turned her back on him.

Water splashed as his bare feet thudded across concrete. She felt her body warm as she listened to him towel off, visualizing his tall bronzed body behind her without a stitch on.

He was certainly taking his time. Was he trying to tempt her into turning around? She *wanted* to turn. Thankfully, she resisted. Surely he'd had time to secure the towel, but another intolerable minute passed.

Finally, as if sensing her impatience and interest in his physique, he chuckled and said, "It's safe for you to turn around now."

But it wasn't. Not when his fierce black eyes devoured her, obviously reading her wicked desires. Not when he wore only that towel and they both knew he was naked and gorgeous and completely male underneath it.

She wished she didn't feel so keenly alive every time she was anywhere near him. She wished she wasn't drawn by his tanned arms and bare chest, that she didn't remember lying with him as a girl after they'd made love and nuzzling that dark strip that vanished beneath the thick folds of his towel.

Oh, how she'd loved him that night after he'd made love to her. Like a foolish child, she'd thought he belonged to her, that he would always be hers.

Maybe he would have—if she'd fought Thurman and the town. Maybe then she wouldn't feel as she did right now, as if she was starving for love.

"You've got guts to come out here all alone. Aren't you scared of what I might do to you?"

Her heartbeat accelerated. She didn't fully understand her motives. She'd just known that she couldn't let him bully her, and that she couldn't stand by and let Tuck be hurt because of her past sins.

Moving closer to him to prove her bravery, she said, "You ran away. Maybe you're the one who's scared of me."

He flushed darkly. "And then again, sweetheart...maybe not."

Sweetheart. The word ripped her heart. In the past, he'd always said the endearment so tenderly it took her breath away. Today, his voice was harsh with irony.

Before she knew what was happening, his hand snaked toward her, and he yanked her against his body, which was wet and warm and as hard as steel.

Her heart leaped into her throat as she caught the faint scent of scotch on his breath. Too late, she wondered how much he'd drunk.

"I wasn't scared of you, you little fool. I was scared of me. Of what I might be tempted to do if I didn't get away from you. Then you come here...and deliberately invade my privacy. You tempt me...into this, into holding you again. Sweetheart, you're playing with fire."

Again too late, she realized he hadn't had time to swim off any of the liquor he'd drunk.

"Well," she hedged, "I...I see you were right.... And I was wrong. Maybe it would be smarter to set up another meeting tomorrow morning, as you suggested."

Echoing her thoughts, he said, "It's too late for such a sensible decision. You came here because you want something from me, and you want it very badly. You saw I was naked. You knew you were alone with me and you stayed. Since I told you I still wanted you, maybe you thought if you excited me again, I'd be easier to deal with."

"No!"

"Hey, don't back down. You were right. It's good for your

cause that you're here. As it turns out, I know exactly what I want from you. I was just fighting the temptation earlier."

*Oh, God.*

"I didn't stay because you weren't dressed…and I thought I could manipulate you…or whatever horrible thing you think I was up to."

His swift grin was savage. "You've always been good at pretending. Like back in high school—when your stepfather bullied you into graduating early, you pretended you wanted what he wanted. He wanted you to be a teacher because he thought that was a respectable career for a woman. Did you ever once tell him how important theater was to you before you starred in *Grease* and made him so angry at the end of your senior year? You dated me behind his back, too, because you knew he wouldn't approve. And when he hung me out to dry, you lied to everybody in this town about me. Your whole life was a lie. So, you'd damn sure lie now."

"No…"

"I think you've gone on lying to yourself for years. You know how I know? Because I've been doing the same thing. In my arrogance, I thought you'd taught me such a bitter lesson I was immune to women like you…and to you specifically. Until I kissed you…."

She swallowed, suddenly not liking the way he was holding her, or the way he was looking at her with that big-bad-wolf grin.

"I'd better go."

"You're so damned beautiful." He was staring at her as if she were a puzzle. "How can you look so innocent? I have enough money to buy practically anything, anybody, I want and I usually do. I want you. Why should I deny myself?"

Drawing her closer, he reached up and gently brushed away the lock of blond hair that feathered against her skin.

Her tummy flipped. Tenderness from him was the last

thing she'd expected, and it caused hot, unwanted excitement to course through her.

He smelled of chlorine and sunlight, scotch and of his own clean male scent, which somehow she'd never forgotten. All of it together intoxicated her.

Her reaction frightened her. When she tried to back away, his grip on her wrist tightened.

"I want you to move in with me for a while. I want to figure out this thing that's still between us."

"Impossible!" He wanted sex. He just wasn't going to say it. "There's nothing between us."

Again, she tried to jerk free, but his hand and body were granite hard.

"You're such a liar. Before we kissed, I would have agreed. I wanted to believe that," he said. "But unlike you, I'm uncomfortable lying to myself."

"I'm under contract in New York. I've got an opening night in eight weeks. We're going to be rehearsing, and I have several scenes to shoot for a movie in L.A. My calendar is full. Crammed."

"So reschedule."

"I have commitments, a life…. Other people are involved. Producers, my director, the rest of the cast."

"Odd—you failed to mention your movie-star boyfriend… Hugh, I believe?" His eyes darkened.

"Yes! Of course—*Hugh*. We're in the same film."

Zach's grim smile held no satisfaction. "And you think I don't have someone special or plenty on my plate?"

*Someone special.*

The thought of him having a girlfriend he truly cared about tugged painfully at her heart—which was ridiculous!

"Even I, who know next to nothing about the theater world, have heard the term *understudy*," he continued. "Reschedule."

"I hate you."

"Good. We're on the same page." His voice was harsh. "You'll live here, with me, weekends only—until your opening night. I don't care how you live the rest of the week. Or with whom. I'll be commuting here from Houston."

"I have to know exactly what you want from me," she whispered.

"I'm a man. You're a woman. Use your imagination."

"This is crazy."

"You forget, I'm a gambler. Ever since you pulled your little stunt and nearly destroyed me, I've gotten to where I am by operating on my gut. If I feel like it's right to go ahead with a deal, I do...whether or not I have all the facts to support my decision. Even if the facts tell me it might be the wrong thing to do—as in your case—I do it. It's worked for me so far."

"This isn't business. I won't have you gambling with my future, with Tuck's future."

"It's the way I operate. Take it or leave it. Since I hold the winning cards where your brother and his band of merry thieves are concerned, I don't think you have a better option."

"Is it sex? Do you want me to sleep with you? If that's it—just say so."

"Sex?" His black gaze raked her. "I won't say that offer doesn't tempt me. Did you mean tonight?"

When she didn't deny it, when she bit her lip and said nothing, he cupped her chin. Again, his hold was gentle, only this time it was more intimate as he studied her, his black eyes lingering on her lips before traveling lower. His hand stroked her throat. When his fingers slid briefly beneath the neckline of her dress, causing her skin to burn and her pulse to race even faster, she gasped in anticipation.

"I want you in bed, but it's not that simple," he finally murmured, removing his hand.

Only after he stopped touching her could she breathe again.

"I want you in bed, but I want you to be willing. So, this isn't just about sex. Not by a long shot."

No, it was about submission, about complete domination and control. She'd read plenty about how ruthless he was. He wanted to humiliate her as thoroughly as he'd humiliated his stepmother.

She shut her eyes because his gaze was too powerful and her own desire was beginning to feel too palpable.

"I loved you," he whispered. "I trusted you, but you betrayed me."

"I…I…loved…you, too."

"Shut up, Summer! You and your stepfather and his cronies nearly sent me to prison. For statutory rape. I was nineteen. Now, any time a reporter shows up here or in Houston to do a new story on me, they dredge up the past. That's not something I'll easily forget. Or forgive—ever."

"But…"

"Even though my uncle got me out of that mess, even though I've made a success of myself, a cloud has hung over my name. For years. No matter how much money I made. Because of you. Do you understand? At the least opportune times, when delicate deals hang in the balance, a belligerent press will hound me about those trumped-up charges, especially because you're so famous now. No matter how high I climb, somebody's always there, wanting to throw me back in the gutter where you put me. So, I came back to this town— to set things straight once and for all. I want to bury the past and silence my accusers. If you move in with me, everybody around here will think you approve of me and always have.

So, yes, this is about more than sex or revenge or whatever the hell else you think."

"You seem to have done okay in Houston."

"No thanks to you! If you'd had your way, I'd be a registered sex offender today. My uncle was at least able to get that part of my record expunged." The rough bitterness that edged his low tone made her shiver.

"Despite what you say, your plan sounds like revenge."

"You owe me," he muttered. "You don't want me to press charges and sic the crazy justice system on your brother, the way you stuck it to me. Because we both know how destructive and long-reaching the consequences for that would be.

If you do what I ask, Tuck gets a free ride. My plane and pilot will be at LaGuardia Airport every Friday at 3:00 p.m. to pick you up and fly you here for as long as your companionship amuses me. Be there, or by damn, I'll forget how beautiful and vulnerable and innocent-looking you are and do as I please with your brother."

"You wouldn't—"

"Are you willing to risk Tuck's future on that assumption? My anger over the way you railroaded me fueled my ambition to achieve all I've achieved. I doubt Tuck will be so lucky if you throw him to the wolves."

She was shuddering violently when he let her go. Still, his burning eyes didn't release her for another long moment.

"And I have one more condition—you're not to tell a soul about our little bargain."

"Don't do this," she pleaded softly.

"If it gives you any pleasure, I feel as trapped as you do," he muttered.

"Then why are you punishing us both?"

"This meeting's adjourned!" he said in a harder tone. "I intend to finish swimming laps. Naked. You can watch me or join me or leave. Your choice."

Grinning darkly with cynical, angry amusement that stung her to the quick, his hands moved to his waist to shed his towel. Even though he took his time, and she had plenty of time to turn away, she stood where she was, daring him.

Like a raptor, his black eyes gleamed diamond hard as he

ripped the white terry cloth loose. With a shocked gasp she watched, mesmerized, as it fell down his long legs and pooled in an untidy heap beside his bare feet.

His tall legs were planted firmly apart as his hard eyes locked on hers. His full, sensuous mouth smiled wickedly in invitation.

Although she willed herself to turn away, he was so uncompromisingly male, so fully aroused, she was too compelled by him not to look.

"Why don't you stay and swim, too? We could start your weekends a week early," he murmured in a low, seductive tone.

Hot color crept into her cheeks. How could just looking at him be so electrifying? If only she could have hidden her admiration. "I...I don't think that would be wise."

"We're way past wisdom," he murmured drily. "You want to. I want you to. We're both adults. You start serving your time, maybe I'll get my fill of you sooner rather than later. I could let you off early...for good behavior."

Tempted, she trembled as she fought the fierce need to move toward him, to touch him. Her hands clenched. Looking at him took her back to the most glorious, sensual night of her life. He was so virile and handsome she couldn't think.

She wasn't that foolish, naive girl any longer. She'd been fiercely independent for years.

But the foolish hopes and dreams of that girl still lurked in her heart, tormenting her. If Summer didn't turn and walk away, or run—yes, run!—she would do something incredibly stupid, something she would regret for the rest of her life.

Just as she regretted their past love.

Only, she didn't feel as if she regretted it anymore.

Why not? What was happening to her?

Did some crazy part of her want to try again? Did she

really want to risk everything she'd achieved for a second chance with him?

*He got you pregnant. When you tried to tell him, he wouldn't even talk to you.*

But how could she blame him for what he hadn't known?

"I see you're unsure," he murmured with a faint, derisive smile.

"I—I'm not unsure," she said even as the burning desire in his eyes made her feel as if she was melting. "I think you're a monster, so I—I'm leaving. R-right now. Really."

He laughed. "Then check with Davis for my phone numbers. Call me if you decide to take my offer so I can tell my pilot and my caretaker. Since I'm a gambling man, I'll wager that you'll be here next Friday. We can swim together then. Or do whatever else we feel like. We'll have the whole weekend to enjoy each other."

He spoke casually, as if her decision meant little to him. Then he turned and walked away.

Her stomach in knots, she watched him much too hungrily until he vanished behind a wall of shrubbery.

# Four

*Manhattan*

Summer loved Central Park, especially on a sparkling September day when the leaves had begun to turn and a cool front had put a chill in the air.

"Hugh, I'm so sorry I can't fly out to L.A. this weekend."

Hunched over her smartphone on a bench near the fountain at Bethesda Terrace during a rare break, Summer chose her words carefully.

Guiltily, she pushed a blond strand of hair out of her eyes. "My brother's in trouble, so I have to go back to Bonne Terre."

"But…"

"Truly, there's nothing I'd rather do next weekend than be with you at the premiere of *Kill-Hard*."

"My agent swears it's my breakout role."

"I'm so sorry. Truly. I'll be there Sunday…late."

*After Zach.*

When Hugh hung up, seething, she was a little surprised that her guilt was overwhelmed by relief.

At least Hugh's premiere was one thing she could scratch off her to-do list.

Summer began to flip through her calendar, deleting or canceling other engagements. For the next few weekends she would be doing her own script work, so she could juggle the commute to Louisiana. Later, when rehearsals began in earnest, getting away from New York would be trickier, maybe downright impossible.

She would worry about that later. Zach would probably be tired of her by then anyway.

Daily, hourly, all through the week, she'd resented Zach for causing such immense upheaval in her life. His demand was outrageous, medieval, and she told herself she was furious with him and with herself for going along with him.

And yet, if that were true, why did her breath catch every time she remembered the avid desire in his eyes? Why did she dream of him holding her close every night? Or awaken hot and sweaty from the image of writhing in his arms like a wanton? She would toss her sheets aside, go to the window and stare out at the stars, imagining spending two days and nights with Zach.

Being a man, no matter what he'd said, all he wanted from her was sex.

But what did she want?

She didn't know. And she didn't know what she could tell Gram. Summer didn't want her grandmother to get her hopes up for no reason. Since she couldn't figure that one out and didn't want to lie, she wouldn't call Gram or take her calls until Summer saw her again in Bonne Terre. Until then, Summer would concentrate on her career goals, on developing and playing her roles. It wasn't healthy to obsess over a man whose sole goal was to punish her.

On Friday, at three o'clock sharp, she met Zach's pilot. Once aboard the jet, she pulled out her script, intending to figure out her character for the scenes with Hugh scheduled to be shot in L.A. next week.

Normally, Summer chose roles because she felt affection for the character, but in this case, her reasons had been more pragmatic. When she'd complained that she didn't think she could do a dark, unlikeable sex addict, her agent had pointed out that the money was simply too good to pass up.

So, Summer needed to study her lines and determine how her edgy sex scenes fit into the emotional context of the movie.

But her mind drifted to Zach, making it impossible for her to concentrate on the femme fatale she was to play in Hugh's film.

Staring out the windows of his Houston office as he held his phone, Zach frowned as his pilot brought him up to date.

"Yeah. She was right on time. Weather looks good until we hit Louisiana. Looks like you're going to have a nasty drive." He gave Zach the plane's arrival time, and the two men ended the call.

Outside, dark purple clouds hung over the city to the northeast. It was only three, but the freeways were already jammed with cars. Impatient, because he'd wanted to leave the city well before rush hour, especially if there was bad weather, Zach thrust his hands into his pockets and prowled his office like a caged cat.

Leroy McEver, the newly hired contractor on Zach's biggest project downtown, was late as usual. Although Zach was sorely tempted to leave, no way was Zach driving to Bonne Terre without making Leroy understand once and for all that the reason he'd fired Anderson and hired him was that he expected Leroy to stop the constant cost overruns.

But even with pressing business to deal with, Zach was anxious to be on his way to Bonne Terre. To her. As always, his inexplicable need to bed her, even after what she'd put him through, annoyed the hell out of him.

After their love affair had been exposed and made to look ugly in the newspapers, he'd zealously guarded his personal life. He kept his private life private. She was a movie star, who probably courted media attention.

There were multiple reasons not to go through with the bargain he'd made with her. But he wouldn't put a stop to it. He couldn't.

Thus, his impatience to see her again infuriated him. He hated himself for stooping to blackmail.

But he wanted her, and she owed him—big-time.

One minute the road was darkly veiled in mist. In the next the brightly lit Thibodeaux house loomed out of the shadowy cypress and oak grove. Summer got out, grabbed her bag and thanked Zach's pilot, Bob, for the lift.

"I've got orders to wait until I'm sure you're safely inside."

Summer's footsteps sounded hollow as she marched up the path, crossed the porch and rang the doorbell.

Setting her bag and briefcase down, she turned the key Bob had given her in the lock, jiggling it until the door opened.

"Zach?"

Again, as her shy, uncertain voice echoed through the empty rooms, she marveled that a man like him, with a house like this, had no staff. As she felt blindly for the light switches on the wall, she heard a man's heavier tread approaching. When she saw a tall, angular shadow splash across the floor between the stacked boxes, her heart began to pound as unwanted, craven excitement coursed through her. All week, she'd waited for this and had been too ashamed to admit it.

"Zach?"

"It's just me, Summer," Tuck said as he ambled through the door at the far end of the room. He had earbuds in his ears and was bouncing to some soundless beat. His hands were jammed into jeans that rode so low on his skinny hips she marveled that he didn't worry about them falling off.

She couldn't see much of his skinny face for the thick golden hair hanging over his eyes.

"You doing okay...since the hospital?" she asked.

"Ever since Zach told me he's not going to press charges, or even fire me, I've been fine. Can you believe he gave me a second chance?"

"Big of him."

"Course, he locked his liquor up and set some pretty strict ground rules," he muttered more resentfully. "Oh, he said I'm supposed to tell you that you can have the bedroom down the hall on the first floor. He made me stock the fridge and get the room ready for you. And he told me to carry your suitcase inside for you."

Tuck came to an abrupt stop in front of her. When she reached for him, he allowed a quick hug.

"I'm glad you're okay," she whispered, ruffling his hair. "Next time, think."

He leaned down and grabbed her suitcase. "Zach told me to tell you about the security system." He told her the code and asked her if she wanted him to write it down or show her how to set it.

She shook her head.

When he showed her the room, she was pleasantly surprised to find antique furniture, curtains and rugs that went together. A silver mirror and comb and brush set lay on a low, polished bureau.

"It's pretty," she said.

"Because Zach sent a dumb decorator and lots of other people over to boss me around and make sure it was."

"Where is Zach?"

"On the road. His meetings ran a lot later than he expected."

"Oh."

"So, why are you here tonight if you hate him so much?"

"I—I don't hate him. It's…it's complicated."

"You're not here because of what I did, are you?"

"Oh, no. It has nothing to do with you." She felt her cheeks heat. "We just…er…reconnected. That's what happens sometimes…with old flames."

He stared at her as if he didn't quite buy it. "So…okay…everything's cool, then. Can I go? I was gonna play some pool tonight before I found out about you and Zach."

She gritted her teeth, not liking that he'd accepted them as a couple so easily. He'd talk, and everybody would believe him.

He stared at her through the greasy strings of his blond hair. "You sure you're okay about this?"

"I'm great! Never better!" She gave him a bright smile.

"You've sure got the whole town talking."

She winced. "You know how people in Bonne Terre talk."

"Yeah. When I shopped for stuff, people kept asking me questions about you."

"So, who are you playing pool with?" she asked, anxious to change the subject.

"Some guys. *Good* guys."

"Hope so. Hey, did Zach say when he'll get here?"

"Maybe. I don't remember. So—can I go now?"

"Give me another minute."

She had work. Lots of it. Since she was a trained stage actress, movie roles did not come naturally to her. Scenes would be shot out of order, and she wouldn't be able to fall back on the rhythm of the play to carry her character into her scene. Since she needed to study the *before* moments that preceded every scene, she should be happy Zach was running late, but, for some reason, the thought of being alone here in his house with her script depressed her.

Making her way into the kitchen, she opened the fridge and found it full of her favorite cheeses, eggs, fresh vegetables and sparkling water. Zach must have talked to Gram to find out things she liked before sending Tuck to get them.

Closing the fridge door, she realized she wasn't going to work tonight when she felt so empty and strange being in Zach's house without him.

"Can I go now?" her brother repeated.

"If you'll give me a ride to Gram's first."

"If I were you I wouldn't go over there. The local gossips really have her and her friends all stirred up about you. She's been hounding me for details. Says you won't return her calls."

She knew Tuck was right, but she'd rather be at Gram's facing hard questions than stay in this house alone, waiting for Zach. On the drive to Gram's, she switched the conversation back to Tuck. "So, how come you agreed to work for Zach again after you got in trouble? Is it the job you like? Or him?"

"The work's boring, but he's okay. Funny, he's almost like a friend."

Her stomach tightened with alarm. Zach was far from a friend. Tuck should have better sense than to trust that man. But there was no way she could tell Tuck that without giving herself away.

"I wish you'd go back to school and find something that interests you. Then you wouldn't have to do boring work. Or work for Zach."

"School's even more boring. And like I said, I sort of like working for Zach."

"Maybe if you tried to be interested, you'd become interested."

"That's what Zach said the other day when he drove me over to the junior college."

"He what?"

"Drove me to the tech campus. In his Lamborghini. Boy, was everybody impressed."

"I can't believe he took the time.... He's a very busy man." She couldn't hold back now. "You know, Tuck, he's not really your friend."

"Hey, where do you get off criticizing him? You're never here. He is." His tone was low as his sad eyes whipped around to regard her. "You're this big famous actress. Until Zach came back to Bonne Terre, Gram and me didn't interest you much. With your glam job, how could you understand what it's like for someone like me, somebody who's ordinary and stuck here? I can't help if it's hard for me to get excited about my life. It's not much to get excited about."

"Then you've got to do something with your life, Tuck."

"I've heard it before."

"If you don't do something, nobody else is going to do it for you. Life is what you make it."

"Easy for a big shot like you to say. Why don't you stay out of my business, and I'll stay out of yours? Deal?"

"No, it's not a deal!"

*Damn.* Because of Zach, she was losing precious ground with her brother.

Refusing to come in, Tuck dropped her off at Gram's. As Summer got out of the car, he sped away in an angry whirl of dust and gravel.

Dreading being grilled by Gram, especially after not taking her calls all week, Summer squared her shoulders before marching up to the house.

Summer was barely inside before Gram switched off the television and plopped Silas down on the floor.

"Why didn't you return any of my phone calls?"

*Because I was too ashamed of what I was doing.*

"That was…unforgiveable of me," Summer whispered. "I did listen to every single message though…if that counts."

"So, when were you going to tell me you've started seeing Zach Torr?" Gram asked excitedly.

"It's not what you think," Summer hedged, feeling acutely uncomfortable that her grandmother was hoping for a true romance.

"What is it, then?"

"Look, it was a long flight. I'm thirsty. Do you have some tea?"

"Why didn't you tell me? Why did I have to hear this from all the gossips?" Gram asked rather gloomily as she and Silas followed Summer into the kitchen.

Summer didn't say anything as Gram splashed tea from a pitcher in the fridge into a tall glass.

"Well, if you won't talk, I'll say my peace. I think it's great that you're reconnecting with Zach."

"We're not…."

"It's high time you two sorted out the past."

"Gram—"

"It will do you both a world of good…to talk it out."

"There's nothing to talk out."

"Oh, no?" After stirring in lemon and mint Gram handed Summer the tall glass of iced tea. "You could talk about New Orleans. And the baby."

Summer's chest felt hollow and tight.

"You looked like death when you came home from New Orleans. I used to wonder if you'd ever get over it. Maybe if you told Zach, let him share that grief with you, maybe then both of you could move on. He's just as stuck in the past as you are."

Summer shook her head. "That was fifteen years ago. It's way too late for us."

Losing his baby after he'd rejected her had hurt so much, Summer had locked her sorrow inside. She'd never wanted to suffer because of it again.

Tears burned behind the back of her eyelids. "I can't talk about it, not even like this, to you, Gram."

Gram's arms slid slowly around her, and Summer, fighting tears, stayed in them for quite a while.

"Spending time with him is the brave thing to do. I think it's a start in finding yourself. I, for one, am going to pray for a miracle."

"You do that," Summer whispered, not wanting to repeat that, for her and Zach, it was hopeless.

"In the meantime, we could play Hearts," Gram said more cheerfully .

"Gram…I…"

"I just love it when Zach stops by to play Hearts…. A man with as much as he has to do taking time for a little old lady… And he's not even my grandson."

Zach again…besting her. Was there no competing with him? No escaping him?

Feeling cornered, Summer sat down with Gram to play Hearts.

Except for the lights she'd left on, the Thibodeaux mansion was still dark several hours later when Summer drove up in Gram's borrowed Ford sedan, after having lost too many games of Hearts. She hadn't bothered to set the security system, so she simply unlocked the door and let herself in.

Feeling restless because Zach still wasn't there, she showered and dressed for bed in a thin T-shirt and a pair of comfortable long cotton pants. Intending to mull over her scenes for a little while, she pulled back her covers and slid into bed with her script.

But just reading through the sex scene made her squirm, so when she saw the remote, she flicked on the television, surfing until she found the weather channel.

There was a big storm over east Texas that Zach would have to drive through. Video of downed trees, traffic signs and power lines made her more apprehensive, so she turned the television off.

Was he okay? If he'd been in an accident, would anyone even think to call her?

*He's fine. Just fine. And why should you care if he isn't?*

Even more restless now, she got up and padded into the kitchen where she poured herself a glass of sparkling water. She was pacing when her cell phone rang. Hoping it might be Zach, she sprinted back down the hall to answer it.

"What the hell do you think you're doing?" Thurman demanded without bothering to greet her. "How can you move in with that bastard? You should be ashamed of yourself."

She *was* ashamed, and furious at Thurman for punching that hot button.

Headlights flashed across the front of the house as her stepfather lambasted her. Stiffening her spine, she stood up straighter. She wasn't some teenage girl her stepfather could blackmail or control.

"How did you get this number?" Summer said. "I've told you never to call me."

"What are you doing over there? I demand to know."

"It's none of your business. And it hasn't been for a very long time. Mother's dead. I'm an adult. Goodbye."

"You're dragging the family down into the dirt all over again!" He swore viciously.

She turned her phone off just as Zach's key turned in the lock.

Thinking she should give him a piece of her mind for putting her through all this, she stomped toward the front door. Then he stepped wearily across the threshold. She registered the slump of his broad shoulders, which looked soaked in the gray light.

"Hi," she said, feeling an unwanted mixture of relief and sympathy for him.

"Sorry." He seemed as tense and wary as she was. "I hope I didn't wake you up."

"You didn't." No way would she admit she'd been worrying about him. "Thirsty." She waved her glass of water. "Thanks for getting all my favorite stuff. For the fridge, I mean."

"All I did was have Rhonda make a phone call to your grandmother. Rhonda's my secretary." When he smiled crookedly, he was incredibly handsome despite the dark circles of fatigue shadowing his eyes.

"Long day?" she whispered, feeling slightly breathless, already having fallen under the spell of his lean, sculpted beauty.

He nodded. "Even before the drive. Long week, too. When it rains…it pours. Literally."

"Oh, and the storm. Was it bad?"

"It slowed me down."

From the late hour and his tight features, she was almost sure that was an understatement.

"Do you have any more bags? Could I help you carry something inside?"

"You're being awfully nice. Too nice," he accused, his dark eyes flashing dangerously. "Why?"

"Yes—and I don't know why. I don't trust myself, either."

When he smiled and seemed to relax, she felt her own tension ease a little. But just a little. After all, their shared weekend loomed in her imagination. She wasn't sure what he expected of her tonight.

"No," he said. "I don't need help. This is all I brought." He paused. "If you hadn't spent your night here waiting on me, what glamorous place would you have been?"

"In L.A., at Hugh's premiere."

At the mention of Hugh, Zach's eyes darkened.

"I was going out there this weekend because we start shooting together next week."

"Are you two doing a love scene?" His voice was hard now. *More than one.*

Annoyed because he'd nailed her and because, like most people, he so obviously attached undue significance to anything of a sexual nature on film, she ignored his question.

"I don't want to talk about Hugh with you."

"Good. Because neither the hell do I."

She hesitated, wondering why he sounded jealous and not knowing where to go from here. "Are you hungry?"

"Look, there's no need for you to worry about me. It's late…. And I've screwed up your schedule enough today as it is."

Of course he was right, but he looked so bone weary, as if it had taken everything out of him to get here while she'd rested on his plane and had been pampered at Gram's.

"I'll just put some cheese and ham out," she said. "You bought it, after all."

"Not so that you would stay up and wait on me. I can take care of myself."

"It won't take a minute," she insisted, stubbornly refusing to let him boss her around.

"Okay. I'll be back down after I freshen up." He left her and carried his bag and briefcase upstairs.

By the time he strode into the kitchen, she'd opened a bottle of wine and set a single place for him at the kitchen table.

When he sat down, she noted that his black hair was still gleaming wet.

"You're not eating?" he said, sipping wine, when she hovered but didn't sit.

"I ate at Gram's earlier."

"Not those chocolate-chip cookies she baked just for me, I hope?" he teased.

"She bakes them for me, too—even though I tell her not to." Summer grinned back at him. As she pulled out a chair, she couldn't stop staring into his utterly gorgeous eyes. Was there a man alive with longer lashes? A tiny pulse had begun to throb much too fast at the base of her throat, causing her breath to catch.

What was going on? How could she actually be so thrilled he was here, safe and sound, when he'd forced her to come to him, when he intended to deliberately humiliate her? When Thurman and the rest of the town were judging and accusing her? When Hugh was sulking in L.A. and her agent and director were apoplectic? When she'd disappointed poor, darling Gram, who was hoping for a happy ending to this farce?

"I had a few cookies after a chicken sandwich," she replied, striving to sound nonchalant. "Dessert is allowed sometimes, you know."

"Even for an actress who has to keep her perfect figure… so she'll look mouth-wateringly sexy in those love scenes… with Hugh?"

His angry black gaze flicked over her breasts in her thin T-shirt. His male assessment accused her even as it made her blood heat.

"Love scenes in movies aren't the least bit sexy. They're all about creating an illusion for the viewer."

"Is that so? You always were good at creating illusions."

He glanced away abruptly, trying to hide his obvious interest in her body and his fury at the thought of her with Hugh, but it was too late. Suddenly the walls of his kitchen felt as if they were closing in on her, and she couldn't breathe. How could he charge the air between them with a mere question and a hot, proprietary glance?

"You have no right to attack me or to look at me like that. No right at all."

"Then maybe you shouldn't dress the way you do," he muttered in a tone so savage she knew he was as provoked as she.

"I'm wearing an ordinary T-shirt."

His hard eyes burned her breasts again. "Right. I guess it's the fact the material's so thin and you're braless underneath that's getting to me."

"Sorry!"

When she felt her nipples tighten and poke at the cotton fabric, she clenched her hands. He was impossible. Since he'd come back to Bonne Terre, he'd been turning everything into some sort of sex game.

"Why you're determined to put us both through a weekend like this, I can't imagine."

He stared at her for a long time. "You know why. Just as you know you have it coming." He stabbed a piece of cheese.

"I think I'd better go back to bed," she said abruptly, not trusting herself, or him, or the intimacy of their cozy little situation. "We're obviously not a couple who can cohabitate easily and naturally."

At her rejection, his dark face was suddenly blank and cold. "Good idea. Go ahead. I'll clean up—alone."

"You're supposed to be a billionaire. Why don't you have staff to do all that?"

"Because they're people, and I'd have to deal with them and their problems. Because I want to live informally here and not be bothered by too many prying eyes. Because I couldn't be here…like this…with you, if I had a staff. Not that I don't have a cleaning lady. And my secretary just hired a gardener. So, do you have more questions about how I live my life before you leave me in peace?"

He wanted *her* gone! She was getting on *his* nerves! His attitude infuriated her. He'd blackmailed her into coming here, hadn't he? He'd launched the blatant sexual attack.

What had she expected—wine and roses?

Her heart pounding, she turned stiffly. Marching to her bedroom, she locked herself in and threw herself on the bed where she lay wide-awake, tossing and turning and staring up at the ceiling for what felt like an endless time.

Her mood was ridiculous. She should be thrilled he didn't want her tonight.

She heard the savage clink of dishes and silver in the kitchen, of a garbage lid being slammed, of the disposal grinding violently. His heavy tread resounded in the hall outside her door and on the stairs. Then he stomped about in the room above hers. Something crashed to his floor so hard she sprang to a sitting position. Fisting her sheets, she stared at the ceiling listening, but after that bit of violence, he quieted.

When he turned on the water, the sound of it hummed in her blood. She imagined him naked in his shower with hot suds washing over his warm, sleek muscles. And despite what he'd said to anger her, she wanted to go up and join him.

Slowly, she got out of bed and went to her bathroom. Stripping, she turned on her own shower. When the water was warm, she stepped into the steam, threw her head back and let the pulsing flow drench her. She cupped her breasts and imagined him seizing her, thrusting inside her. She imagined her hands circling his hard waist. She imagined pressing herself against him even tighter as she begged for more.

The water ran down her limbs and circled in the drain. Sighing in frustration, she fell back against the tile wall while the spray streamed over her. A strange sensation of loss and a fierce longing to move beyond their past and their present darkness possessed her.

She clenched her fists, beat the tiles, but it did no good.

He disliked her, yet he would force her to stay with him.

Did he intend to hook her on his lovemaking and then laugh at her and leave her? Would he flaunt their relationship to everybody in Bonne Terre and beyond to prove she and her stepfather had wronged him?

She closed her eyes and pushed her wet hair out of her face. Because of her own shameless desire, she was on emotionally unsafe ground.

How would she make it through the weekend without falling more deeply under his spell?

# Five

When Summer awoke the next day, she sat up slowly, her heart racing, as she thought about Zach upstairs in his own bed. Except for the birds, the house seemed too quiet and dark. But that was only because she was used to pedestrians on the sidewalks and tenants on the stairs, to sirens and traffic, to garbage trucks making their early rounds as the Upper West Side woke up.

Fearing Zach might not have slept any better than she had, she crept noiselessly from her bed to the bathroom where she brushed her teeth, washed her face and combed her hair.

Rummaging through her suitcase, she put on a T-shirt and a pair of tight-fitting jeans. Okay, so he'd probably comment on how tight they were, but she didn't own any other kind.

Grabbing her script, she headed for the kitchen where she found a bag of coffee. She closed all the doors before she ground the coffee and started a pot. Listening to the birds, she decided it might be more fun to work on the porch.

She went to the door and was taking great pains to open it without making the slightest sound, when the security alarm began to blare.

With a little scream, she clamped her hands over her ears and fought without success to remember the code.

"Blast it!" she muttered as Zach slammed down the stairs.

Wearing nothing but a pair of jeans, and dragging a golf club, he hurled himself into the kitchen.

"My fault. I forgot about the alarm," she said, staring at his chest and finding him heart-throbbingly magnificent. "I was trying so hard not to wake you."

He punched in the code and set the golf club down. "It's okay. Usually I get up way before now. Coffee smells good." He raked his hands through his hair.

"It does, doesn't it?" She broke off, tongue-tied as usual around him, maybe because his gaze left her breathless.

"Did you sleep okay?" he asked in a rough tone.

"I guess."

"I had a tough night, too," he murmured, grinning sheepishly.

His super-hot gaze made her tummy flip. Suddenly, sharing the kitchen with him when he was sexily shirtless, when he kept his eyes welded to hers, seemed too intimate. She felt as awkward as she would have on a first date when she knew something might happen but didn't know what. Quickly, she turned away and poured herself a coffee. Then she scurried outside. Behind her she heard his knowing chuckle.

Not that she could work out here, she mused, not when he was bustling about in the kitchen.

*Concentrate on something else! Anything else but him!*

The morning air was fresh and cool, and the sky a vivid pink. As her frantic gaze wandered to the fringe of trees that edged the far corner of his property, three doe and a tiny fawn picked their way out of the woods in a swirl of ground fog to nibble a clump of damp grass.

Summer tiptoed back to the kitchen door and pushed it open. Holding a fingertip against her lips, she waved to Zach to come out.

When he joined her, he smiled, as charmed by the scene as she.

"I'll bet you never see anything like that in Manhattan."

"There are all sorts of amazing sights in Manhattan," she murmured in a futile attempt to discount the awe that sharing the dawn with him inspired.

"I'll bet somebody as famous as you could never live anywhere as boring as Louisiana or Texas again. Or be serious about anybody who wasn't a movie star like Jones."

"I didn't say that!"

His hard eyes darkened as they clashed with hers.

An awkward minute passed as she tried to imagine herself living with Zach, here, in Houston, anywhere. Impossible—she was an actress, who lived in Manhattan.

"To change the subject—what do you want to do today?" he asked casually.

"I need to study those scenes I have to shoot next week."

"That's fine. I did make tentative plans for us to meet Tuck and Gram at the new Cajun café on the bayou. Over lunch I thought we could encourage Tuck to enroll in one of the tech programs at the junior college."

"Tuck's not interested in school."

"Really? When I informed him I might press charges if he didn't take some responsible action about his future, he told me he'd like to take some courses that could lead to a career as a utility lineman."

"I can't believe this! You're threatening Tuck, too, now."

"It's way past time he stepped up to the plate. I took him over to the junior college Wednesday and introduced him to Travis Cooper, who's the young, enthusiastic head of that particular program. He was a late bloomer, like your Tuck, which may be why the two of them hit it off immediately."

"Okay—I can do lunch," she replied. "I like your results, even if I don't approve of your tactics. Then I'll need to study my scenes this afternoon…since I procrastinated last night."

"Okay. While you do that, I'll inspect one of my building projects."

He took a long breath, his black eyes assessing her with such frank male boldness her tummy went hollow. "But, I'll want to spend the evening with you. Alone. Here."

"Of course," she whispered, her skin heating even as she fought to look indifferent.

Without warning, he stepped closer and grinned down at her. "I'm glad you agreed so easily. I want you to be eager."

He bent his handsome black head toward hers, and she was so sure he would kiss her, she actually pursed her lips and stood on her tiptoes as if in feverish anticipation.

But he only laughed, as if he was pleased he had her wanting him. "Save it for tonight, sweetheart."

A very colorful curse word popped into her mind, but she bit her lips and made do with a frown.

Lunch with Tuck and Gram was amazing. First, the succulent fried shrimp, which were crunchy and light, were so addictive Summer had to sit on fisted hands to keep from stealing the one Zach left on his plate just to tempt her. As she was staring at that shrimp, Tuck finished his gumbo and astonished her by informing Zach that, yes, he'd decided he was fine with giving Cooper and his dumb program a chance. She was further amazed when she listened to him converse easily and intelligently with Zach, as Tuck rarely did with her. She could tell that Zach really had been devoting a great deal of time to Tuck, and that Tuck was lapping up the attention.

Despite all that was enjoyable about lunch, she didn't like the attention from surrounding diners, who stared and snapped pictures with their phones.

"Did you have an ulterior motive for lunching with all of us so publicly?" Summer asked after they dropped off Tuck and Gram and were driving home.

Zach's mouth was tight as he stared grimly at the road. "Being railroaded on felony charges and then being tried in the court of public opinion wasn't any picnic, either."

"That still doesn't make it right for you to use Tuck and Gram to get even with me."

"Maybe I just want people to see that I have a normal relationship with all of you," Zach said.

"But you don't. You're blackmailing me."

"Right." His dark eyes glittering, he turned toward her. The sudden intimacy between them stunned her. "Well, I want people to know that you're not afraid of me. That you never were. That you liked me, loved me even. That I was not someone who'd take a young, unwilling girl off to the woods to molest her. Is that so wrong?"

His face blurred as she forced herself to focus on the trees streaming past his window instead of him. The realization of how profoundly she'd hurt him hit her anew.

Yes, he'd hurt her, too, and yes, he'd gone on to achieve phenomenal success. But he'd never gotten over the deep injury her betrayal had inflicted—any more than she'd gotten over losing him and the baby.

Because of her, Zach had been accused of kidnapping and worse. All he'd ever tried to do was help her.

When a talent scout had been wowed by her high-school performance in *Grease,* her stepfather had forbidden her to go back to her theater-arts class. He'd sworn he wouldn't pay for her to study theater arts in college, either.

So she'd run away to Zach, who'd forced her to go back

and try to reason *with Thurman.* Only after her stepfather struck her and threatened her with more physical violence if she didn't bend to his will had Zach driven her to Nick's fishing cabin on the bayou in Texas. There they'd hidden out and made love. There they'd been found in each other's arms by Thurman and his men.

She did owe Zach. More than a few weekends. And not just because of Tuck. If Zach wanted to be seen with her and gossiped about—so be it.

"You don't have to drive me home before you go to your site," she said softly. "I'll go with you."

"I thought you needed to work on your love scenes with Hugh."

His voice hardened when he said the other man's name, and she felt vaguely guilty. Which was ridiculous, since she wasn't in a relationship with either man.

"I do, but I'll study on the plane, or later, when I get to L.A."

"Well, if you're coming with me, I've got to take you home anyway. Those sandals won't work at the construction site and neither will that tight, sexy skirt."

"Oh."

"You'll need to wear a long-sleeved shirt, jeans and boots. I'll supply you with a plastic hard hat and a safety vest with reflective tape."

"Sounds like a dangerous place."

Even though it was Saturday, cranes, bulldozers and jackhammers were operating full force as battalions of workers carried out all sorts of tasks, none of which made sense to Summer as she adjusted the inner straps of her hard hat. Zach seemed as happy as a kid showing off as he led her around the site, pointing at blueprints, sketches and plans with a pocket roll-up ruler, introducing her to all of his foremen and contractors. Local men, all of them, who eyed her with open speculation.

Zach was developing hundreds of acres along the bayou, creating a dock for his riverboat casino, as well as restaurants, a hotel, a small amusement park, shops, a theater, a golf course and no telling what else.

"I've never built anything," she said, "so I'm impressed. Look, you don't have to entertain me. I'll explore on my own."

"You be careful and don't go too far."

At first she stayed close to him because the ground was rough and muddy. Then she began walking toward the dock on two-by-fours that men had laid across deep holes as makeshift bridges.

She was standing on such a bridge when Nick drove up in his battered pickup, looking for Zach. The elderly shrimper wore faded jeans, a T-shirt and scuffed boots. Even though he dipped his cowboy hat ever so slightly when he saw Summer, his cold, unsmiling face told her he hadn't forgiven her. Until Zach's uncle had shown up, Nick had been Zach's sole advocate.

"Didn't expect to see the likes of you here, *cher*," he said when he walked up to her. "Dangerous place for a woman."

Nick was thinner than the last time she'd seen him, his tanned skin crisscrossed with lines, his wispy hair steel-gray. But the penetrating blue eyes that pierced her hadn't changed much.

"And you're a dangerous woman for any man, even Zach. I warned the boy to stay away from you, but he won't listen," Nick said, eyeing Zach, who stood a hundred yards to their right, deep in conversation with a contractor. "He never did have a lick of sense where you were concerned. I don't like you settin' your hooks in him again. By coming out here with him you'll have the whole town talkin' and thinkin' you're a couple again."

"Tell him. He invited me for the weekend."

Nick spat in disbelief. "Well, you tell him I stopped by and that I'll catch up with him later. Or, if he'd prefer, he can drop by…after he gets rid of you."

She nodded.

He turned and left.

Her mood dark and remorseful, she headed toward the dock. Because of the deep holes in the ground, she was forced to cross on the makeshift bridge again. She'd nearly reached the dock when Zach called out to her.

Maybe she turned too fast—one of the boards slipped, and she tumbled several feet into the muddy hole filled with rocks and debris. When she tried to stand, her left ankle buckled under her weight.

She looked up in alarm and saw Zach running toward her, his dark eyes grave. Leaping over the boards, he was soon towering over her. "Are you okay?"

"Yes—except for my left ankle."

"I should never have brought you here."

"Nonsense. I fell. It all was my fault."

"Hang on to me, then," he commanded, jumping down into the hole.

Half carrying her, he led her out of the pit and back to his car. As he drove away from the site, he called Gram, who recommended her doctor, a man who generously offered to meet them at the emergency room. Dr. Sands actually beat them to the E.R., and Summer, who'd once fallen off a stage in Manhattan and had waited hours in a New York E.R., was both appreciative and amazed to be treated so quickly and expertly in such a small hospital. Most of all, she was grateful to Zach for staying with her.

When a team of nurses stepped inside the treatment room and asked him to leave, Zach demanded to know what they planned to do.

"Dr. Sands wants her to disrobe for an examination, so we can make sure we don't miss any of her injuries."

"But it's only my ankle that hurts," Summer protested.

"Hopefully you're right. But this is our protocol. We have to be sure."

Summer reached for Zach's hand. "Would you…"

So, he stayed beside her, gallantly turning his back when they handed her a hospital gown and she began to undress. But once, when she moaned, he turned. She saw his quick flush and heard his gasp before he averted his gaze from her body.

Her stomach fluttered. Funny that it hadn't occurred to her to be embarrassed that he should see her almost naked. She simply wanted him beside her.

When the professionals finished checking her body and stooped to examine her ankle, she cried out in pain.

Zach was at her side, pressing her hand to his lips. "Hang in there. We'll be home before you know it."

*Home.* How sweetly the word buzzed in her heart. She squeezed his fingers and held on tight, feeling illogically reassured.

He was right. In less than an hour she was back at Zach's house, propped up on his couch by plump pillows, surrounded by his remotes, her script and her favorite snacks.

Strangely, after the hospital, there was a new easiness between them. Gram and Tuck had stopped by to check on her, and after they departed, Zach remained attentive, never leaving her side for long. He said he wanted to be nearby in case she needed anything. She found his hovering oddly sweet and realized it would be much too easy to become dependent on such attentions.

When the sun went down, he cooked two small steaks and roasted two potatoes for their dinner while she watched from her chair at the kitchen table. They had their meal with wine and thick buttered slices of French bread out on the back veranda.

Again she marveled that a man who must be used to servants knew his way around in a kitchen. She didn't mind in the least that he hadn't thought to prepare more sides. The simple meal was perfect even before the three deer reappeared to delight them.

Later, when she was back on the couch again and he'd finished the dinner dishes, he pulled up a chair beside her. Pleased that he hadn't gone up to his room, she declared the steak delicious and thanked him for his trouble.

"I'm not much of a cook," he said. "Eggs, steak and toast. That's about it."

"Don't forget potatoes. Yours were very nice. Crispy."

"Right. Sometimes I can stick a potato or two in the oven and sprinkle them with olive oil and salt. I have a cook in Houston, but I don't like eating at home alone. So, mostly I eat out."

"Me, too. Or I do take-out. Because I don't have time to cook."

"I imagined you in ritzy New York restaurants, dining on meals cooked by the world's best chefs, eating with famous movie stars."

When his expression darkened, she suspected he was thinking of Hugh.

"Not all that often. Fancy meals take time to eat…as well as to cook and serve," she said, avoiding the topic of Hugh. "And fans pester you for autographs. Besides, there's nothing quite like a homemade meal, is there?"

"You used to want to be an actress so badly. What's it like now that you've succeeded?"

"It's nice, but I work almost all the time. Even when I have a job, I'm always auditioning for the next part. When I sign on with a show that isn't in New York, I travel and live out of a suitcase. One minute it's a crazy life, full of parties and friends, then it gets pretty lonely. You can't hold on to anything because it's all so ephemeral. The friends I make within a cast feel closer than family for a while. Then they vanish after each show closes," she admitted.

"But when you sign with a new show or film you have a new set of friends."

"Yes, but as I get older, I see that, despite the bright lights, a life without stability isn't nearly so glamorous as people think."

"It's what you wanted."

She sighed. "Be careful what you wish for. I guess I took my real life for granted. Lately, I've realized how much I miss family…and roots."

"What does that mean?"

"My job is so all-consuming that I…I haven't been good at relationships. I'm Southern, like Gram. She sees my single state as a failure, and lets me know it every chance she gets. Her dream for me was marriage to a handsome husband. I was supposed to have two children, a boy and a girl, and live happily ever after in a cute house surrounded by a white picket fence."

He smiled. "But you, being a modern woman, aren't into such an outdated, traditional formula for happiness. Strange, that it can still exert such a hold over a female as wise as your grandmother."

"You're right, of course. I just wish I could make her understand that I have everything I set my heart on. I'm grateful for what I have, for what I've achieved. So many people would give anything to be me."

She was saying the same truths she'd lived by for years, but, for some reason, the words felt hollow tonight.

Zach didn't say anything.

She'd never imagined having such an ordinary, simple,

companionable evening with him, and she found herself enjoying it more than she'd enjoyed anything in a very long time. When they'd been kids, they'd been friends before they'd been lovers. They hadn't fallen in love until after he'd graduated and she'd been entering her senior year.

Now, as an adult, she spent so much time working on her image and her brand, so much time learning various roles, and never very much time being herself. What would it be like to have a lifetime of such evenings with a man like him? To take them for granted?

She sighed. That wasn't who she was now. She had her career, a bright future—and it was on the stage and screen.

"What about you?" she whispered. "You're successful. Are you happy?"

"Like you, I'm not unhappy," he muttered thickly. "I, too, have everything I always thought I wanted…except maybe for…" He shot her a look that was so intense it burned away her breath.

"For what?"

"It doesn't matter," he growled. "Not even billionaires can have it all. Not that we don't pretend that we can, with our fancy cars and homes and yachts." Frowning, he sprang to his feet and then glanced at his watch. "But you're injured, and it's late. You must be tired. Besides, Sands prescribed that painkiller. I'm afraid I've been very selfish to keep you up so long."

She didn't want him to go. "No. I'm barely injured, and you've waited on me hand and foot…. And I just sat there and let you."

"Well, I won't keep you any longer."

"But I really do want to know…about you," she whispered.

"Let's save that boring tale for later," he said, cutting her off. "Who knows—maybe you'll get lucky and never have to hear it." He picked up her crutches. "Why don't I help you to your room?"

Feeling stunned and a little hurt by how abruptly he'd ended their pleasant evening, she got to her feet. As she stood, her uncertain eyes met his. But he wouldn't hold her gaze.

Suddenly, she again felt awkward at the thought of their sharing the house for another night. Stiffening, he handed her the crutches and then backed away.

"I hate these things," she said as she placed the crutches under her arms.

"It's a minor sprain. The doctor said you might even be off them as soon as Tuesday."

"I hope so. Thanks again for tonight. When you convinced me to come here for the weekend, I never thought…we would have this kind of evening or that I could enjoy simply being with you so much."

"Neither the hell did I," he admitted in a stilted tone, still not looking at her. "Believe me—I had a very different kind of weekend in mind."

"Well, you've been very nice."

"Good night, then," he muttered, his voice sounding so furious she realized he'd had more than enough of her company.

He'd blackmailed her because he'd wanted revenge. He'd wanted sex. Had this evening, with its simple pleasures, bored him?

She felt hurt and rejected, just as she had last night.

# Six

Zach knew he wouldn't be able to sleep for a while, so instead of undressing for bed, he poured himself a glass of scotch. Then he strode out onto the balcony where the humid air smelled of honeysuckle, jasmine and pine.

Damn those bewitching blue eyes of hers and her pretty, sweet smile that made him want her so badly he hurt.

Why hadn't he taken Summer as he'd intended? Why hadn't he punished her? Usually he came on strong with women. What the hell was wrong with him this weekend?

Next week she would be with Hugh, making love to him—at least on film. And probably offscreen, too. Not that her relationship with Jones should be any concern of Zach's. Still, he burned every time he thought about her with that egotistical phony.

Their first night here she'd seemed so vulnerable and uneasy. Then today, when she'd fallen, she had taken his hand and begged him to stay with her. Her fingers and wrist had felt so slim and fragile in his much larger hand. What kind of man forced his presence on a woman who seemed so defenseless and in need of his protection?

Still, Zach wasn't so noble that he could forget the glimpses he'd seen of her breasts and her creamy thighs. He wanted to kiss those breasts, tongue all the warm, succulent places between her thighs. He knew what she'd done in the past, how close she'd come to nearly destroying him—but for reasons he didn't understand, he continued to balk at using her sexually.

No longer did he want to expose their relationship to the press for public consumption.

This weekend had backfired. Damn it.

The sensitive male was a new role for him.

She'd beaten him.

To save his own ass, tomorrow he'd tell her their deal was off and send her packing.

Then he'd do the smart thing: return to Houston and forget her.

The next morning, when Summer awoke, her ankle was so much better she could almost walk without limping if she used one crutch. When she went into the kitchen she discovered that Zach had already cooked and eaten breakfast. She looked down at his dishes in the sink and realized he was avoiding her.

Rolling the scrambled egg and bacon he'd left for her into a tortilla, she walked outside and saw him swimming laps in his pool. When she waved, he got out.

As he dried off, it was all she could do not to stare, even though he wore swimming trunks.

His eyes were guarded as he strode up to her. "How's the ankle?"

"Much better," she whispered, lowering her lashes.

"Good. Bob is standing by to fly you to L.A. So, whenever you're ready, just call him. I know you've got work, and so do I, so I won't keep you."

He was so remote and cool that her acute disappointment and hurt felt like withdrawal, which was ridiculous.

"What about next weekend?" she whispered, her voice catching. "Do you still want to see me?"

Zach sucked in a breath. "Like you said, maybe spending the weekends together wasn't such a good idea. So—you won." His voice was cold, revealing nothing.

He slung a towel across his shoulders and turned away, dismissing her as if she were of no importance to him.

"Are you mad at me?"

"Yeah. Mad at myself, too."

"Zach..."

"You have your real life...in the theater. And I have mine. I think we should just cool it."

He was right, of course.

"Or maybe not," she said huskily as she focused on his profile. "I want to know why you blackmailed me and then changed your mind, why you were so nice last night and are so cold today."

"Maybe I started thinking about what happened fifteen years ago and don't see this going anywhere positive."

He wasn't making sense. Last week he'd wanted to punish her. And now... What did he want?

"What if I disagree?" she whispered. On impulse, she leaned forward on her tiptoes and kissed his rough cheek tentatively.

When he jerked away as if burned, she beamed. "I enjoyed last night, you see. Too much. And I thought maybe you did, too...just a little. You were sweet."

"Sweet?" He almost snarled the word.

She smiled gently. "And I thank you for what you're doing

for Tuck, too…taking him out to the tech school and all…
especially after what he did to you."

"Forget it," he snapped.

"What if I can't?"

"Soon you'll fly to L.A. to film those love scenes with
Jones. Don't waste your charm or blatant come-on sexuality
on me. Save it for him."

"I don't care about him."

Not believing her, he scowled.

"I don't."

When she edged closer and held her hand to his face, Zach
froze. At the first light touch of her fingertips on his warm
throat, he shuddered. When he tried to wrench away, her
hands came around his neck so she could hold him close.
She had no idea what she was doing or why she was doing
it, she only knew she didn't want to part from him so dis-
passionately, when something new and wonderful was beginning in her heart.

"Can't you at least kiss me goodbye," she whispered, too
aware of her taut nipples pressing against his hard, bare chest.

"Not a good idea," he growled.

"You sure about that?" She rubbed her hips against the
hard ridge of his erection, sighing as her body melted against
his.

On a groan, he reached for her, gripping her with strong,
sure arms, pulling her close, like a man who was starving
for her.

She was starving, too, starving for the intoxicating sensu-
ality of his mouth claiming hers. He tasted so good, so right.
For fifteen years, she'd wanted this and denied it. Why should
she fight it now? Moaning, she kissed him back.

His savage grip crushed her. His hungry passion ignited
unmet needs. Murmuring his name feverishly, her fingertips
ran through his thick, inky hair.

"All weekend I wanted this," she whispered. "Wanted you. Wanted to touch you, to kiss you…to be in your arms…even though I tried to tell myself I didn't. Friday night I lay in bed, wanting this more than I'd ever wanted anything. And last night after we talked, I craved it even more, craved it so much I felt like I was about to burst. Then you went upstairs, and I felt so lost and alone in that bed. I—I couldn't sleep for hours. You told me you'd make me want you, and you were right."

"You shouldn't say these things."

"I don't understand any of it and yet…it's the truth."

"Hell," he muttered. "This isn't some damn role you've got to understand. Life's messy and chaotic and doesn't make a lick of sense most of the time. Like now. Like last night. I decided you're the one woman I should have nothing to do with. And yet here I am…."

"Tell me about it," she whispered. "You're definitely bad for me, too."

When his mouth took hers again, his desperation and urgency made her dizzily excited.

"This is crazy," she whispered as her fingertips glided across the damp hair on his bronzed flesh. "I didn't want to come this weekend, and now I can't bear to go."

"I don't want you to go, either."

"Punish me like you swore you would. Make love to me," she whispered.

The next thing she knew, he was lifting her, kissing her wildly as he carried her up the stairs, into the house and then down the hall to her room. Locking the door, he drew her down to the bed.

In no time, she stripped, but even in her rush, she enjoyed the striptease, for never had she played to a more fascinated audience. He lay on the bed watching as she undid her blouse in the shadows. Button by button, her slim fingers skimmed downward. He held his breath, his eyes burning when she threw her blouse aside and unhooked her bra.

"You are exquisite," he rasped when she slid her lacy panties down her thighs. Vaguely she was aware of him rustling with a foil wrapper. Then, reaching for her, he lay down beside her and buried his face in the curve of her neck.

She let her head fall back, offering him her breasts. "You're pretty okay yourself."

His lips traced the length of her throat. He tasted first one nipple and then the other until they beaded into damp, pink pearls. She trembled with an enjoyment she couldn't hide, which she could see excited him even more.

When his lips found hers again, she fell back against the pillows and opened her mouth so his tongue could slide inside.

"Strip for me," she whispered. "I want to see you naked."

"Wicked girl."

Grinning, he ripped off his swimming trunks. Her breath stopped. He was huge and gorgeous, magnificently virile. While she watched approvingly through the screen of her lowered lashes, he tossed his trunks into a far corner.

Reaching toward him, she slid her hand over his manhood, circling it so that he inhaled sharply. While she touched him, he caressed her most secret, delicate folds with bluntfingered hands, teasing her sensitive nub of flesh until her breath came hard and fast and she wanted him inside her more than anything.

But he refused for a while longer, teasing her with his mouth and hands while she grew hotter and wilder.

How had she lived without him all these years?

Squeezing him, she rubbed in an urgent, methodic way until he groaned and gathered her close. She heard the sound of a foil wrapper again. Then he slid the condom on and, much to her delight, positioned the head of his shaft against her damp entrance.

Murmuring her name, he hovered there, kissing her hair, her brow. Only when she arched her hips upward in sensual invitation did he slide all the way inside. For a moment, he stopped and simply held her so they could savor the sensation of their joined bodies.

"Zach," she pleaded.

His hips surged. She cried out as he drove himself home.

Their eyes met and held. With her hands, she cupped his face and kissed each of his cheeks and then his nose.

He sighed, as if relieved of some immense weight. Then, all too soon, some primal force took over.

How she loved lying underneath him, staring up at the breadth of his bronzed shoulders, at his black hair that dripped perspiration onto his gorgeous face as he pumped. She felt on fire. With every thrust he claimed her, and she surrendered to him as she had as a girl, completely, irrevocably, giving him every shattered piece of her heart.

Thus did he sweep her away to emotional and sensual peaks she'd never known before. Crying out in the end, she held on to him, feeling lost and yet found again as he exploded inside her. In a blinding flash, she saw that he had always remained at the center of her heart.

For a long time she lay trembling quietly beneath him. Then she kissed his damp eyelashes and eyebrows. *I love you,* she thought. *I always have. This is what has been missing.*

*If I have everything else and lack this, I can never be complete.*

Only gradually did she grow aware of how wonderfully heavy he was on top of her. When she opened her eyes and looked up at the hard angles of his handsome face, she saw that he was staring down at her with a brooding intensity that frightened her.

"You've got to go soon, so you can cram for those damn scenes with Jones." Frowning, he kissed the tip of her nose.

"Yes," she replied drowsily without the least bit of enthusiasm. "I think you just sapped all my ambition to be a movie star. I just want to stay here with you."

He nipped her upper lip a little firmly…as if to snap her out of her languid mood. "But that's not who you are, is it? You said your career is what completes you, not relationships. And with my uncle not there to help me anymore, I've got a helluva lot to do in Houston. So…"

No sweet words. Nothing. Just those two parting kisses.

A chill swept her. Had she been wrong about their sex being spiritual as well as physical? Had it just been revenge for him after all? Now that he'd had her again, was he done?

"And next weekend?" she murmured, deliberately keeping her voice light. "Do we meet again?"

"I'll call you," he said slowly, but there was no conviction in his voice. Her heart sank as he stroked her neck absently. "Like I said, we both have a lot on our plates."

"Sounds to me like maybe I'm off the hook. For good behavior?"

"Maybe," he admitted.

"Okay, then. I get it."

He stared at her, sucked in a breath, but didn't reply.

She rose, reached for her clothes and began to dress hurriedly.

So what if he wasn't going to call? She'd served her time, so to speak. Now he wouldn't press charges against Tuck.

Logically, she knew that it was probably best if this thing between them ended here. For her, sex with him had been too intense, too all-consuming for her to have a light affair. He would break her heart all over again if she wasn't careful. No smart adult should let herself become involved with a man she'd loved and obsessed over for years.

But she wasn't feeling logical. She was feeling sensually

and emotionally aflame after his lovemaking. The whole world seemed aglow. He seemed a part of her, her other half.

Naturally, she wanted to see him again, to lie in his arms like this again. She felt she'd lose a vital part of herself forever if she couldn't. Which meant he'd completed his mission, by using sex as a weapon to punish her.

He'd won.

# Seven

On her flight to L.A., try as she might, Summer found it impossible to concentrate on her script. Hurt simmered inside her because of Zach's coolness at their parting. Thus, the minute the jet's wheels slammed against tarmac, she turned on her phone, desperate to check her messages.

She swallowed when she found only a single text from Hugh.

can't meet u. nominated sexiest man n known universe 2day. jerk leaked information about hot scenes n dangerous man. horde of paparazzi @ my bldg.

No sooner had her plane rolled to a stop in front of a private hangar than a herd of photographers stampeded her jet.

*Great. I'm on my own. This is what I deserve for letting the world think even for one minute I was ever serious about Hugh.*

Bob stuck his shaggy head out of the cockpit and said, "Not to worry. I've already notified security."

When she finally left the jet, with a security detail, paparazzi on motorcycles chased her limo all the way to her hotel. Apparently, Hugh's premiere had been well-received by critics and the public, so for now he was the hottest talent in La-La Land.

*Welcome to Hollywood,* she thought as she bolted herself into her hotel room.

When room service arrived with her breakfast the next morning, Summer found a weekly tabloid tucked under her door along with a note from her agent. The tabloid's banner headline read: Sexiest Man In The Universe Teams With Reputed Lover, Broadway Actress Summer Wallace, To Shoot Super Sexy Love Scenes. The article beneath the headline made her feel cheap and tawdry, especially after her weekend with Zach.

Summer Wallace upset legions of fans this weekend when she failed to attend the premiere of *Kill-Hard* on the arm of rumored lover, Hugh Jones, star of the film. Instead, the actress tiptoed into the city late last night. It's no secret their fans can't wait for a sneak peek of their favorite couple out on the town together this week. Or better yet, a sneak peak of those love scenes in *Dangerous Man*. We hear they're going to be sizzling.

Her week got crazier, but what made her *feel* crazier was that Zach never called or texted.

When she was on the set, Summer didn't know if it was the soul-stirring sex she'd shared with Zach or Hugh's sulky attitude toward her after she'd told him she'd reconnected with Zach over the weekend, but filming intimate moments with Hugh was awkward. She was tense, Hugh impatient and their director, Sam, who called for endless takes, apoplectic.

It didn't help her mood that every male employee in production made up some pretext to show up on the set to leer. During the most intimate scenes, she felt as if she was betraying Zach. Even though he'd dismissed her and had shown no inclination to see her again, she worried about what he'd think of the finished film. Not that she or Hugh had to strip for the camera—in fact, she had a clause in her contract that protected her against nudity.

By day two she felt as if she was playing Twister with a sullen, male octopus. Whatever spark had ever existed between Hugh and her was absolutely dead. The only way she endured her scenes with Hugh and managed to respond in character was to remember how she'd felt when Zach had touched her or kissed her.

She wanted Zach, but his silence made her that wonder if her longing was one-sided. At night, when she was alone in her hotel room, hoping Zach would call, she felt lost and lonely and under more pressure than ever.

By Thursday, they were forced to film late into the night. Just when she thought the endless, excruciating takes on that satin bed would never end, Sam yelled it was a wrap. He was thrilled with the rushes.

"You were fantastic, Summer," he said. "Gorgeous in every shot. Every man in America will envy Hugh."

For the first time in her career, she didn't care about that. She just wanted to be with Zach. Even though it was pretty obvious Zach didn't feel as she did, Sam's praise reawakened her concerns about how Zach might react to the movie.

Relieved to be finished, Summer headed back to her hotel. While she was showering, her phone rang. She grabbed for a towel and then her cell. She could see from the number that it was Zach.

"Hi," Zach said as she pulled the towel around her dripping body. "How's the ankle?"

His voice sounded so hard and cold, she wondered why he'd even called.

"Actually, I'm not on crutches anymore. So, it's great...." Her voice died into nothingness.

"Glad to hear it. So—you won't sue me," he murmured drily.

She held her breath, waiting, hoping his mood would lighten, hoping he'd called to say he wanted to see her again.

"I called to say I decided not to let you off for good behavior after all."

"Oh." She stopped, stunned, wondering where this was going and whether his motive stemmed from the need to punish or the desire to be with her.

"There's a ground-breaking ceremony tomorrow—Friday night—at my construction site. My PR people think I need a date, and they think you'd be the perfect one.... You being a celebrity and a hometown girl. Since you still owe me, I decided to call. You'll need to dress up and look beautiful—movie-star beautiful."

So this wasn't about them; this was about his work.

"But you've already broken ground. I mean... I fell in that hole, didn't I?" she said softly, hoping he would admit to feeling more for her.

"Won't happen tomorrow night because I'll be holding on to you all night long. Good for my image."

Her hopes and his tension warred in the silence that hung between them. She was a big girl. She should be used to men wanting her only for publicity.

"The whole town will be there," he said. "So, a fringe benefit of this appearance will be having the gossips around here see that you don't view me as a threat. I know this is late notice, but you do owe me."

"Of course, I'll be your date," she whispered.

When he didn't say anything, she realized anew how tense he was. How could he have made love to her so passionately and then have turned so cold? It was as if he'd turned off a switch and now disliked her more than ever. How could she have been so wrong about what they'd shared?

To keep him from hanging up, because some tiny part of her believed she hadn't been wrong, she said, "So—how've you been all week?"

"Fine." Again his voice was too abrupt.

"Work went okay?"

"The usual challenges. And your scenes with Hugh? How did they go?" As always, when discussing the subject of Hugh, his tone hardened. Which was strange—he'd been so aloof since they'd slept together. Why would he care?

Maybe she should explain about how grueling and unsexy the work had really been. Maybe she should tell Zach that because of him, she'd ended it with Hugh. But she didn't want to discuss Hugh, not when Zach was in his present dark mood. Not over the phone.

"Sam, our director, says he's happy. I'm…I'm just glad the week's over. After Bonne Terre, it felt like the four longest days of my life…because I…I missed you."

She willed him to say he'd missed her, too, to say anything…. When he didn't, she chewed at the edge of a fingernail.

"Zach…"

"Hmm?"

She took a deep breath. Why was it so impossible to talk to him now when it had been so easy the night after her fall?

"Never mind," she finally said. "I'll see you tomorrow."

"Tomorrow," he repeated sternly. "Bob will call you and

set a time and place to pick you up." He hung up after an impersonal goodbye that left her feeling emotionally dissatisfied.

If only he'd sounded the least bit eager to see her.

He'd called, hadn't he? He'd demanded that she spend another weekend with him.

Maybe she'd given up on them too soon when she'd been younger. She didn't want to make the same mistake a second time.

"There's no such thing as bad publicity." That's what Zach's PR guys said. They loved that somebody had stolen the hot love scenes from Summer's new movie and plastered them all over the internet.

Zach disagreed. Tension fisted around his lungs as he studied the stolen clips of Summer with Jones. She was so gorgeous he couldn't breathe. Even though she was lying beneath another man, just the sight of her sparkling eyes, tremulous lips, breasts and silken hair got his pulse thudding violently. In an instant, he remembered her looking at him exactly that way and how nauseatingly vulnerable he'd felt when he'd realized there was no way he could make love to her again without surrendering his heart. In one stolen weekend, she'd gotten through every careful barrier he'd spent years erecting, which made her too dangerous to fool around with.

Since there was no way he was ever giving her his heart again, he'd sent her packing.

But that hadn't stopped him from wanting her.

Hell. She'd plunged him back into hell. That's what she'd done.

Within minutes of starting the clip, he'd seen more than he'd ever wanted to see of Summer on those satin sheets. Did she have to moan under that egotistical actor just as she had when Zach had made love to her last weekend?

*She was just acting.*

*Or was she?*

*Maybe she'd been acting in Bonne Terre, in Zach's bed.*

It didn't matter.

He damn sure hadn't been acting. He'd been wildly upset that he'd felt so much more than lust for her; furious that he'd experienced the same shattering, soul-deep bond he'd felt for her as a kid.

He knew too well the destructive power of those emotions, so he'd known what he'd had to do. She'd acted hurt when he'd dismissed her, and that had gotten to him, too, but then she was an actress.

He'd lived without her before. He could do it again.

But then, when he'd been missing her the most, his PR guys had come up with the idea to invite her to the ground-breaking, to put a positive spin on an old story by dating her.

His PR guys had handed him an excuse to see her again. So, he'd broken his vow to himself and called her. He'd told himself it was business; it would only be for one night; they'd be in public. He had no intention of sleeping with her again. He'd be safe.

But he'd been lying to himself. He'd called her because he wanted her.

Damn it, he wanted her so badly he couldn't think ratio-nally. Even as he'd willed himself to forget her and move on, he'd spent the week fantasizing about her lips, her wide eyes, her sweet, responsive body. He'd remembered the same soft expression on her face that he'd just seen captured on film.

He'd been suffering serious withdrawal from his weekend with Summer Wallace.

Zach wished to hell he could cancel her flight. But it was too late for that now. She was already in the air.... Probably an hour away. Bob had said they would run into bad weather west of Louisiana. The last thing Zach wanted was to distract Bob when he was flying during a storm.

He knew it would be a mistake to see her again. Even though his PR guys were even more adamant that he court her after the internet clips were released, Zach wanted to make the smart move and avoid her.

He hated the way she tore him in two. Hated the way he'd felt so out of control, during sex and ever since.

He clenched a fist. He knew one thing for sure. Tonight, after the ground-breaking, he would end it for good.

# Eight

As soon as Zach's jet landed on the narrow tarmac nestled between tall pines outside of Bonne Terre, Summer bent over her phone and frowned. She saw dozens of texts and voice-mail messages from Sam and several other producers of *Dangerous Man,* but none from Zach. Gram and her agent had left messages, too. What was going on?

First, she called Sam, who began ranting about pirated scenes and a lunatic Brazilian hacker, before she could even say hello. He spit out words so fast she could only catch half of what he said.

"But how could this have happened?" she demanded after she finally understood the gist. "And what are you going to do about it?"

"Somehow the kid hacked into my laptop, that's how, damn it," Sam yelled. "I've got firewalls. She's fifteen! That little hacker gave away everything. For nothing! Just 'cause she's got the hots for Hugh. She's cost us millions. Maybe cost me my job. She's denying it, of course, but we've got her IP address."

After more of the same, Sam finally wound down and hung up.

Oh, God, had Zach seen the video? With grim foreboding, Summer listened to Gram's message.

"Everybody's been telling me about some love scenes you're in…. What's going on? Call me!"

Of course, Zach had seen them. Taken out of context, the scenes might look pornographic and might compromise the integrity of the movie, not to mention her integrity as an actress. Summer felt violated, but her main concern was how Zach would interpret those scenes.

With a heavy heart, she listened to Gram's second message.

"You swore to me you weren't going to take off all your clothes. And what about Zach? Everybody says you're his date tonight. Call me."

She hadn't been nude. A double had been used in the only nude shot.

Press coverage had caused tension at home before. Why couldn't Gram learn not to believe all the lies that were printed about celebrities to sell newspapers?

It would be nice to have understanding and support from those who loved her and really knew her. But, no, those closest to her were as easily manipulated by the press as everybody else.

Feeling very much abused and in no mood to explain herself to anyone—not the town or even Zach—she shut her phone off and buried it in the bottom of her purse.


Thibodeaux House was so dark she could barely see it among the trees when Bob dropped her in the drive.

As she was heading up the walk, he called after her. "Hey!

Zach just sent me a text. He'll be here at six to pick you up for the ceremony."

Fumbling with the keys Bob had handed her, she let herself into Zach's shadowy house and unset his alarm.

Had Zach seen the pirated scenes? Did he think the worst of her?

Of course, he did. And he was furious, no doubt.

Carrying her bag, she went to her room and threw herself on the bed. There she lay, hugging herself, as she listened to the birds and the creaks of the old house as the light went out of the sky. She knew she should get ready, but she felt too weary to move.

Finally, after what seemed an eternity, she heard Zach's car on the gravel drive. She ran to the window and watched him walk grim-faced toward the house.

The front door opened and slammed. He strode briskly into the kitchen. When she heard his heavy tread on the stairs, she sat up warily. He hadn't even bothered to check on her.

As if he read her mind, he stopped. She held her breath during that interim before he headed back down the stairs.

Finally, he rapped his knuckles on the door.

"Come in," she whispered brokenly.

He flung the door open and stared at her across the darkness, his blazing eyes accusing her. When he flipped on the light, she sat up, brushed her fingers through her hair.

"Not ready I see." His voice was hard and clipped.

"I was tired," she whispered.

"I can well imagine." His black eyes glittered coldly.

"I didn't know what to wear…. Or if you'd still want me to go with you…."

"Not go when everybody in Bonne Terre is so anxious to see you?" he said in a low, cutting tone. "Not that you left much of yourself to the imagination."

"I can explain…."

"I'm sure—but why bother? Besides, my PR guys are thrilled. They say all your internet coverage is great for Torr Corporation."

He walked over to the luggage rack and unzipped her suitcase. After rummaging through her clothes, he yanked out a low-cut, ruby-red gown that a personal shopper had bought for her in L.A. before she'd known about the pirated love scenes.

"Wear the red. Perfect choice," he said. "You'll look the part your legions of fans expect you to play. And you'll be gorgeous beside me, which is all my PR people care about."

But what did *he* care about? Whatever it was, it was devouring him alive.

"Zach, I haven't seen the videos, so I don't know exactly what you saw…. But I was acting."

"Save it! I'll be back down in a minute!"

"Please—I can explain…."

"Sorry. I don't have time for one of your offscreen Oscar performances. Although you're good—very good. And you were even better last week—in my bed."

He slammed the door in her face and was gone. As she listened to him stomp up the stairs, her heart constricted so tightly she was afraid it would shatter into a million tiny pieces. So, he didn't care how she felt at all.

"You'll get through this," she whispered to herself. "You've gotten through worse."

But had she? She'd never gotten over him…. Or their precious baby.

*Don't think about that. You'll go crazy if you do.*

Zach didn't speak to her on the drive over, and he looked so grim and forbidding she decided it was wise to give him time.

She had done nothing wrong. She'd done her job. Actors acted. She hadn't made love to Hugh for the camera. Her character had. She didn't even like Hugh. It wasn't her fault someone had stolen the video.

Something told her Zach's mood went deeper than jealousy.

The glow that hung over the trees ahead of them brightened as they neared the construction site. When they reached their destination, Zach parked and helped her out of the car. She drew in an awed breath.

The construction site looked nothing like it had last weekend. Transformed into an enchanted fairyland, it was lit by a thousand lanterns. White tents covered dance floors and a dining area. Champagne was being served by a dozen bartenders. Warm laughter and music drifted through the happy crowd. A podium had been set up in front of a thousand chairs.

No sooner had he stopped his Mercedes than reporters and photographers surrounded them.

Taking her icy hand, Zach led her into the thick of the paparazzi where they were blinded by flashes.

His expression fierce, Zach gave the screaming horde a brief statement and posed beside her for more pictures. Then he'd had enough. She hardly knew how he managed it, but with a wave of his hand, his own people led them past the press and into a cordoned-off area where the music and laughter died. For a full minute, she clung to Zach's arm, while he braved this fresh crowd gaping at them with stunned expressions.

Before those prying eyes, she began to tremble, feeling the same guilt she'd known fifteen years ago when these same people had thought the worst of her and Zach.

"Easy," Zach whispered against her ear as he placed a protective hand over hers. Then he signaled his contractor and the band, and the music resumed.

*We've never done anything wrong,* she thought. *We were wronged.*

Slowly, people turned away and began talking once more. Still, even though Summer held her head high, she felt their lingering interest too acutely; just as she felt the steely tension emanating from Zach's hard body beside her.

Never had she been more conscious of having a spellbound audience. During the politicians' speeches and the ceremonial breaking of the ground with shovels, people couldn't stop staring at her and Zach.

She couldn't let their stares matter. All that mattered was Zach.

Maybe he was furious at her. Maybe he felt utterly betrayed. Never once did he leave her side, but perhaps he was putting on a show for the public. Would he make such an immense effort to show his support merely for publicity reasons?

He even danced with her beneath the softly lit lanterns and moonlight, holding her close, swirling her about while all she wanted was to run home and have him to herself so she could explain.

Instead, he forced her to brave the curious, fawning crowd, forced her to stay until all the important guests and photographers had departed. Only then did he whisper in her ear, in a tone that chilled her to the bone, "The crowd has lost their appetite to devour you. Time for us to go home, sweetheart, and start our weekend."

Once they were out of the area that had been cordoned off from the paparazzi, the horde chased them to his Mercedes.

A microphone was shoved in her face. "Is Torr your man now?"

"No comment," snapped Zach as someone snickered.

"When do you plan to make up your mind, Summer?"

Summer felt a jolt as Zach shoved a reporter aside so he could open her door.

A flash went off in her face, blinding her as Zach raced around the hood.

He jumped behind the wheel. "Get your head down. There are cameras everywhere."

"I thought this was what your PR guys wanted."

"Yes, they're probably thrilled."

A moment later, he sped out of the parking lot with the pack tailing them. Inside his Mercedes, which was lit by the headlights of the paparazzi, Zach was fiercely silent behind the wheel. So fierce, she thought his anger had built during the opening ceremonies. She didn't dare say a word during that endless drive through that tunnel of trees to his home.

No sooner were they at his house than the photographers circled them, snapping photographs and yelling questions again.

Zach put his arms tightly around her, shielding her face, and escorted her inside.

"I can see that after this, I'm going to have to build a wall and hire guards to protect my privacy," he muttered once they were in his living room and had drawn the drapes.

"What did you expect, when you asked me to come here as a publicity stunt?"

He double-bolted the front door and turned on her.

"Okay. I got what I deserved—in spades. The PR junket is over. Tomorrow I want you gone. They'll soon forget."

"No, you and I know they never forget."

"Well, I intend to forget. Bob will fly you wherever you want to go. My only request is that you and your bags are on the front porch at 8:00 a.m. That's when I told Bob to pick you up. Do you understand?"

She nodded. "Why won't you even let me explain?"

"I'm sure you could explain your way out of hell itself, but I'm not interested in hearing it."

"What about Tuck?"

"I won't press charges."

"You just want me gone? Out of your life?"

"That about sums it up."

"Zach, please—"

"Save it for your true loves—the stage and the press." He turned on his heel and headed to his room. When his door slammed, she sagged against the wall as he banged about upstairs.

"But they're not my true loves," she whispered. "Not anymore."

In fact, sometimes, such as now, being an actress felt like hell. She was a human being, a woman, whose privacy had been invaded and whose work had been exploited to serve as lurid entertainment for a mass of strangers on the internet. They'd hurt her, but it was Zach, and his refusal to hear her explanation, that ripped her heart out.

An hour later, Summer felt worse than ever as she closed her laptop after having viewed the pirated clips.

The integrity of the film had been compromised by allowing those provocative scenes to be viewed out of context. She felt used and abused as a woman, as well.

She did look wildly enthralled in the videos, but those hadn't been her real emotions.

After the connection they'd shared last weekend, she'd worried about Zach's reaction. Maybe she should have explained what was involved in filming sex on-screen for a major motion picture before she'd left for L.A. She should have made it clear that it was work, hard work…. That it was far from a sensual experience. But Zach had been so cold and forbidding.

Well, she had to talk to him now; had to do whatever was necessary to make him listen…. To make him understand that they had a bond worth fighting for. She wasn't about to leave him again without doing so. That's what she'd done fifteen years ago.

Her heart was beating too fast as she pulled on her robe and headed up the stairs. In her anxious state, it seemed that every stair creaked so that he had plenty of warning to throw the bolt against her.

Much to her surprise, when she twisted the knob and leaned against the door, it opened.

She saw the bottle of whiskey on the table beside the bed. A crystal glass glimmered in his clenched hand as he stood by the window.

"Zach, I'm not going until we talk...."

He whirled. "What do you want now?"

"You. Only you."

"Get out, damn you."

"You'll have to throw me out, because I'm not leaving on my own. Not until you let me explain."

"There's no need."

"You're being unfair...like Thurman and the people of Bonne Terre were to you fifteen years ago."

"And you!" he said. "You were the star of that public farce, too!"

His words felt like blows.

"I was sixteen. Thurman had been running me so long, I didn't know what to do."

"Except stand by him and sell me out."

"I—I never intended to hurt you. The whole thing just got out of control. All I know is that I don't want to lose you again."

She pushed her robe off her shoulders, indifferent as it slid down her arms and pooled on the oak floor. She stood before him in a shimmering, transparent nightgown.

"Last weekend you made me feel so special when you made love to me. I hoped it might be a new start for us," she whispered, feeling fearful because he was so cold and determined to shut her out.

"Did you now? Well, there is no new start for us. There never was, so put your robe back on and get out."

Even as his harsh tone ripped through her, she stepped farther into the room, shut his door and then locked it. She was shaking when she flipped off the light. "You'll have to make me," she said softly, refusing to lose her courage.

"Don't think I won't." Slamming his glass down on the windowsill, he stormed across the room and seized her by the shoulders. "Listen to me—this ends now!"

She put her arms around his waist, lifted her eyes to his, then laid her head against his chest and clung.

He stiffened.

"Please! Don't do this," she begged, even though she felt desperate that he might push her away. "Last weekend…being with you…meant everything…. Don't let the press's distortions destroy us."

"Stop it," he rasped even as he shuddered from her nearness.

Her breath caught. She could tell he wanted her every bit as much as she wanted him, but he was fighting his emotions. Maybe because he didn't trust them, or her.

"I can't. Not until you hear me out. When I saw you at Gram's that first day, all those weeks ago, something started between us again. At least it did for me. Maybe it never died. I didn't want to admit it. I had my career, and that was enough. Then you kissed me… And then we made love. Now none of what I had before you is ever going to be enough. I…want you so much. So very much. Even though I live a crazy life that leaves no time for relationships, I want you."

"What about Hugh?"

"I told you—there's nothing between Hugh and me now except for a little chemistry on the screen and whatever fantasy lingers in fans' minds. We never really dated. I became involved with him after Edward, my boyfriend, walked out on me publicly. I knew the press would focus on Hugh instead of my failure with Edward because Hugh loves media attention and encourages it. It seemed less invasive because it was false. Now I see I shouldn't have used him like that."

"Those love scenes between you two were pretty hot. When I saw you on those satin sheets, looking up at him the same way you looked up at me, something snapped."

His face was closed; his eyes had gone flat and dark. She could tell there was a lot he wasn't telling her.

"I...I can't even begin to imagine what you felt. I only know that if I saw you give another woman that special smile or look, I'd feel betrayed. Foolishly, I thought I'd be able to explain about the love scenes before you saw them...since *Dangerous Man* won't come out for nearly eight months." She paused. "I'm afraid I was thinking about you, when I was with Hugh in front of the camera."

"I don't much like hearing that." His black eyes impaled her from beneath his dark brows.

"I know it was wrong, but I was turned off by Hugh and my selfish, seductive character. It was the only way I could get the work done.... So, in a way, I did use you...use us.... But it's hard for an actress not to use parts of herself to make a role convincing. Our tools are our own emotions."

"Does the acting ever stop?"

"Yes. Now. This is me, and I'm begging you to give me— to give us—another chance."

Terrified, feeling naked to the soul after asking this of him, she inhaled a long breath and waited as he considered what she'd said.

"I don't know," he said finally, but the anger had gone out of his voice. "Since I was nineteen, when everything I read about us was distorted and used to hang me, I've worked hard to keep my private life private. There were, of course, always those reporters who wrote new stories about what I'd supposedly done to you, but mostly my life was a private affair.

"I've never dated a famous actress before. Frankly, I never wanted to. But here you are—a bomb that's gone off in my life. If we date, your career, with all its fuss, is going to take some getting used to."

"I know. I'm sorry about that."

"I thought I had my life under control. It was simple. It was all about building and developing and making more money. Then I lost Uncle Zachery. And I saw your tear-streaked face and kissed you on Viola's porch."

"See—your work is not so different from my roller-coaster career. Until that kiss, I lived for interesting parts and good reviews and felt like death when some critic said I couldn't act."

"I don't like feeling out of control—or in your control."

"That's understandable because I hurt you before," she whispered.

"I don't want this…you…us," he growled. "You're bad for me."

"Not according to your PR guys," she whispered with a smile.

Zach took a deep breath. For a moment, she was terrified that her little joke would backfire, that he was still going to send her away. She wouldn't have blamed him.

But he smiled. "I should never have listened to them."

"Were they really the only reason you called me?"

"Point taken. No… But I wish I could say they were. Then maybe I could resist you."

"That's not the wisest course," she whispered.

Very slowly, his arms gentled upon her shoulders. Wrapping her closely against him, he drew her to his bed and pulled her down onto the mattress beside him. For a long time they just lay together in the darkness growing comfortable in each other's presence.

His nearness calmed her and made her feel safe again.

Then he rolled on his side and began to stroke her lips, her ears, her neck—and lower.

"All night, at the ground-breaking, I was so miserable... because I knew you were going to send me away again." Her words were muttered shatteringly against the base of his throat, her hands clinging to his shoulders.

His hand traced the length of her spine.

"I thought that this second chance was over before we'd even begun to understand what we feel," she continued.

"I damn sure wanted it to be over. You're like a dangerous drug, and I'm an addict."

His hands were smoothing her tumbled hair out of her eyes. His lips kissed her brow lightly. Then he pulled her fully against him, so that she was pressed against his long, hard length. Again—he felt so right.

While he petted her hair, she poured out the details of her past week in a jumble—the male members of the crew jamming the set to ogle her, a dissatisfied Sam shouting commands, the alienation she'd felt every night in her lonely L.A. hotel room when she'd longed for him to call.

"I know people think I have a glamorous life, but sometimes it just feels lonely. One minute I'm onstage admired by thousands. Then I'm home alone—or vilified in the press." She buried her lips against the warm hollow of his neck. "Edward couldn't stand my crazy life, and I don't think you will be able to stand it, either. I'm good at acting, at fantasy onstage. But so far, ever since we parted fifteen years ago, I've never been able to hold on to anything real."

"Just promise me you won't act when you're with me," he said roughly.

She nodded.

"I don't want to look at your face and wonder if you're

using an emotion you felt for someone else to make something work for us."

"I'd never do that."

"Okay, then." His mouth fastened on hers with a passion that soon spiraled out of control. He stripped her, stripped himself and flung their clothes on the floor. Then he mounted her, his knees wide. Straddling her thighs, he cupped her breasts.

She ran her hands down his lean torso. How she loved the way his body was hard and warm; how every part of him was gorgeous.

He breathed in rapid pants, and she was just as hot for him.

He kissed her with such desperate urgency she could only imagine he felt as she did. A foil wrapper rustled. Then, with his condom in place, he thrust inside her, each stroke deeper and harder than the last. She clung, arching her pelvis to meet his. Relentlessly, he took her higher and higher until, at the end, he clutched her close. When he shuddered and ground his hips against hers, she cried his name again and again, her release glorious.

For a long time afterward, their bodies spent, they clung. An hour or so later she awoke to find herself still wrapped in his arms. Never had she felt closer to anyone.

*This is where I belong,* she thought, refusing to consider the secrets she still hadn't told him.

Some time later he began to kiss her with a feverish need that fueled her own desire into an instant blaze. He licked his way down her slim body, exploring secret feminine places until she felt she was so hot and tremulous even her bones might melt.

*Don't stop,* she thought. *Don't ever stop....*

After she recovered from the most shattering climax of her life, he made love to her again. Then they napped and made love again, and maybe again. She lost count.

Needs she'd never experienced before made themselves known. Their bodies spoke to each other in a dark, sweet language only they understood. They said things and did things they'd never done before. Things they could only do now because trust was building between them.

They played erotic games, with tied hands and blindfolds. Sometimes their love was rough, but mostly it was gentle. For an endless time, Summer lived in a sensual universe she shared only with Zach. It was nearly dawn when she drifted to sleep in his arms once again.

She felt changed, as if she'd been reborn within the dazzling magic of his love.

At eight o'clock sharp, his phone and doorbell rang at the same time.

They sprang up groggily, laughing when they realized it was morning.

Zach grabbed for his phone, cursing when it wouldn't stop ringing.

"It's Bob! How the hell could I have been so crazy as to ever tell him eight?"

She giggled. "You wanted me gone, remember."

"Strange how that seems a lifetime away."

He spoke much too curtly to Bob then, who said he was surrounded by paparazzi.

"Poor guy," she said after he hung up.

"I'll apologize. But later. He's too busy keeping the screaming horde at bay." Zach's gleaming eyes met hers sheepishly. "Now that we're up, we might as well make the most of it."

"First, I'm going to go downstairs and take a shower, brush my teeth...present a more civilized—"

He laughed and grabbed her hand, preventing her from squirming across the sheets and running downstairs. "I don't want civilized! I want the wicked wanton I had last night all over again, only wilder."

"Not possible."

"I'm going to prove to you that you're wrong. You're going to stay right here where you belong. Under me. In my arms."

Unable to deny him anything in that moment, she lay back and waited for him to again turn their world into a fiery wonderland that was theirs alone.

# Nine

**Summer Wallace Steps Out With Billionaire Zach Torr!**

"What the hell do you think you're doin', boy?"

Nick slapped a newspaper with the two-inch headline onto Zach's desk, covering the blueprint he'd been studying.

When Zach looked up, Nick began to read him the article in a low, sarcastic voice.

"It seems the thirty-one-year-old actress known for her light comedy roles has revamped herself. Shortly after pirated film clips from *Dangerous Man* exploded all over the internet, Wallace was seen on Torr's arm at the ground-breaking ceremony for his new casino. The couple has a scandalous history. She once charged Torr with—"

"What is this? Read-aloud time?"

Zach wadded the paper and pitched it into the trash. "I've seen it already. Read it already."

And he'd been sickened to have the most beautiful thing in his life described in such cheap terms.

"You said you saw her again for the publicity, yes? Was her two-day sleepover a publicity stunt, as well?"

"That's my business, and hers—not yours! And certainly not the damn newspapers'!"

"Then date another woman."

Zach's voice was meticulously polite. "Look, I intend to. In the future. Right now…I'll be seeing more of Summer."

No way in hell could he give her up now.

"Tell me you've got more sense than to start up with her again. You know as well as I do that she's a liar to the core of her rotten soul, yes? You had to sneak around with her in high school because her step-daddy thought you was trash. Then look what they done to you, those high-and-mighty folks, first chance that they got."

Zach remembered too well. He still wasn't sure about what had been real back then between him and Summer. Hell, he wasn't sure what was real now. But he wanted to find out.

"People don't change, boy. She's probably stepped on a lot more folks to get where she is. You gonna end this or not?"

*Or not.*

Since he couldn't reassure Nick, Zach fixed his gaze on the blueprint. The tension between them built until Martin knocked on the door of the trailer.

"Pete's here," Martin said. "He thinks he sees a way to get what you want done and not go over budget."

"Great." Zach turned on Nick. "I'm busy as hell. I've got things to do here. The costs on a project in Houston are going through the roof, so I've got to fly home ASAP. You and I— we'll catch up later, okay?"

"I'm not finished here, no. That little gal proved what she was fifteen years ago, yes. All that she ever worries about is what's good for her. She don't care about you. She never did. She never will."

Flushing with dark embarrassment to have interrupted his boss's personal conversation, Martin backed out of the trailer.

Zach's face grew stony. "Look, Nick, I've dated a lot of women since Summer. Can't a guy fool around?"

"Not with her, you can't, no. You're not just playing with fire. She's nuclear."

Zach clenched his fist around his pencil, letting go of it right before it snapped. "You're right. You're right."

"Which is why you're madder than hell, yes."

"Stay out of this, Nick."

Grabbing the blueprint, Zach stormed past Nick and out of the trailer.

*"No! No! No! Earth to Miss Wallace!"* Paulo, Summer's stage director, was bouncing up and down as he bounded toward her, his face purple.

"You still haven't got it! Quit thinking about your personal love triangle and listen to me!"

Summer blinked first. Then she blushed. She was sick of the ceaseless teasing she'd had to endure due to all the news stories.

"Sorry." Rubbing her forehead, she fought to concentrate on what Paulo was saying.

Paolo was actually a very insightful, inspiring director, one of the rare ones who really understood actors. Still, it wasn't easy for her to take direction. She was too worried about her fragile new start with Zach and about how she would tell him about the baby. She was concerned about how all the media attention impacted him, as well. Again, the sex had been glorious. Again, she'd felt she'd shared everything with him in bed. But once they'd separated and the stories about them had hit full force, he'd erected the old walls between them.

So, she was no closer to feeling the time had come for her to confide in him.

He'd called her once, texted her twice. All three times her heart had leaped with joy. Even as his husky, but oh-so-controlled tone had made her remember all the thrilling things they'd done to each other—against the wall, on the floor, in the bed, on the chair—she'd sensed his emotional withdrawal.

In Bonne Terre, after their night together, she'd felt so close to Zach. He'd seemed easy, open. But now he was unreachable. Really, she couldn't blame him. He wasn't used to life in a fishbowl. He'd said he'd hated the stories that had linked them for years.

Rehearsals were difficult during the best of times and trying to give birth to a character could be exhausting. Summer's head, back and feet ached from the effort. Distracted by Zach and the media storm, she'd found the rehearsals this week to be sheer torture.

She would think about him and break character, lose her bearing. Another actor would say a line, and she would just stare at them, lost. The entire cast was out of patience with her, as she was with herself.

She needed to get a grip before she sabotaged the show completely. At night, when she was alone in her apartment eating takeout, her obsession was worse.

She would try to imagine living with Zach as an ordinary couple in a house with a garden and a picket fence, try to envision holidays with Gram and Tuck, dinners with friends, shared vacations, dark-haired children that looked just like Zach.

But, always, her vision would pop like a bubble as an inner voice taunted her.

*Zach has his life and you have yours. You're still keeping your secrets. He values his privacy, and you can never have total privacy. So—just enjoy what you have now.*

An affair such as theirs couldn't last long, not with her se-cret eating at her and the world interfering and them living so far apart, not with each of them working at all-consuming careers. Added to those obstacles, there would be no way for her to leave New York on the weekends once her show started.

She thought of Gram, who was always pressuring Sum-mer to marry and have children, who now called constantly to express her pleasure at Zach's renewed visitations and to express her concerns about how their story was playing out in the media and around Bonne Terre.

"You are running out of time for children," she would say. "He isn't."

"Gram, please...don't!"

Gram's advice added unbearable pressure to Summer's already fragile situation.

Until Zach, Summer had focused only on her career. Now when she thought of the possibility of little darlings and a more private life, she felt an eager wistfulness.

What if Zach wanted children but saw her career and all that went with it as obstacles too large to surmount? Since he was a man, he could simply enjoy her for as long as it was convenient and then move on. He could choose a woman young enough to bear his children.

An urge to see him again and to make love to him—to claim him in all the imaginative ways he'd taught her—filled her.

By Thursday night, when he hadn't called her again, she finally weakened and picked up the phone.

"I've missed you," she whispered the minute he answered, fighting to keep the tension out of her voice.

*Oh, why did I say that of all things?*

"I missed you, too," he admitted, his tone polite.

"I'm sorry about all the press coverage."

He said nothing.

"I saw where you were besieged in your Houston office."

"I didn't realize you were so famous." He didn't sound happy about it.

"Hey, you're the handsome billionaire. I think your money and your looks are as big a draw as I am. It's a huge part of the fantasy reporters are trying to sell."

"Oh, so now it's my fault, too," he mused, but his voice had warmed ever so slightly. "When I couldn't get into my building downtown for all the reporters, I wondered why the hell I'd ever gotten myself into this mess. It seems so cheap… what they write about us. Maybe we should take a break until all the fuss dies down."

When he fell silent after dropping that bomb, her breath caught painfully. For a long second, the wound from his words seemed too hurtful to bear.

"Zach, I…I hope you don't really want that. I know the press is a major hassle right now, and I'm truly sorry. But once my show starts, I'll be too swamped to travel. You'll get busy with other projects, too…. And then we'll…drift apart…." Her voice cracked on a forlorn note.

"I've lived in the spotlight for years. It won't always shine this brightly or be this invasive. I swear."

"That's reassuring," he said in a smart-aleck tone that somehow cheered her.

"My PR people spend a lot of time manipulating my brand. It's all so false. The person you read about in those stories is not me. It's this pubic person, the actress. The real me often feels lost in all the hubbub.

"But there is a difference. Last weekend, after the groundbreaking, was wonderful and true. I've never been happier in my whole life."

"Me, too," he admitted slowly.

"So, will you give us another chance?"

"Sweetheart, who am I kidding? Don't you know by now,

that no matter how much I hate the press, I'd go crazy if I didn't see you again—and very, very soon. I need you, even though I hate needing you. But that doesn't kill the need. It's fierce, unquenchable."

She drew in a long, relieved breath because she felt the same way.

"I'm new to this, too," she whispered. "I haven't dated anyone outside the business before. Maybe we should only worry about how we are together…so that those on the outside don't matter quite so much. What we have shouldn't be about them or what they think. It should be about us. I want this piece of my life to belong to me and to you and to nobody else."

He was silent for a long time. "We do live in the real world, you know, an intrusive world."

*A world that would devour them all over again if it learned all their secrets.*

"I know. But I want to try to keep our relationship a personal matter. There are things I need to share with you…. Personal things I've been afraid to share…."

"You sound very mysterious all of a sudden."

"I can't talk about it over the phone. So, about tomorrow… Do we still have a date?"

When he hesitated for a heartbeat, he put her in an agony of suspense.

"I can't wait," he admitted in that low, husky tone she loved.


Friday afternoon came at last, and she rushed to LaGuardia in a chauffeured car with a single bag. Hours later, when his jet set her down on a deserted airstrip several miles from the one Bob usually used outside Bonne Terre, she saw him— and no press—waiting beside his Mercedes at the edge of the dark woods. A wild joy pierced her.

Stepping off the plane, she told herself to play it cool. But at the bottom of the stairway, she cried his name and flew into his arms.

"I missed you so much," she admitted ruefully as she flung her arms around his neck.

He pulled her to him, folded her close.

"You smell so good," she whispered.

He slanted a look down at her and smiled. "So do you."

Feeling the fierce need to taste him, she pulled his mouth down to hers. Then he kissed her with a wonderful wild hunger that turned her blood to fire, the ferocity in him matching her own. Suddenly, it didn't matter that he'd barely contacted her last week or that he'd had so many doubts about their very public relationship. Even the unbearable weight of her secret felt a tiny bit lighter on her heart. There was truth in his kiss, in his touch, a truth he couldn't hide.

"I brought you something."

Soft white flashed in the darkness as he handed her a bouquet of daisies.

"They're gorgeous." She jammed her nose into the middle of their petals and inhaled their sweetness. "Simply gorgeous. I love them."

"It's a cliché gift."

"I don't care."

"You've got gold dust all over your nose now."

"Pollen, they call it," she whispered as she dabbed at her nose and giggled. "All gone?"

"Not quite." He dusted the tip of her nose for her.

Then he wrapped his arms around her and held her close in the shadows of the trees. After another kiss, this one brief and undemanding and tender, he said, "Let's go home, sweetheart."

The press corps waiting for them at his pillared mansion were held at bay by a team of security guards, so Zach drove around back where they could run inside without having to face questions.

Locking the door of the little sitting room where they'd entered, he pulled her into his arms and kissed her hard. So urgent were his kisses as they skimmed her lips, her throat, her breasts. She began to tremble violently. Then he lifted her skirt and found that soft place in between her thighs.

"You're not wearing panties, I see."

His tongue made contact and she gasped.

"No...."

She was wet and breathless and dying for more as he peeled off the rest of her clothes.

"Am I bad?" she whispered as he undid his belt and began tearing off his jeans and shirt.

"I like bad."

When they were naked, he shoved her against the wall and held her close. "Wrap your legs around me, sweetheart."

When she complied, he put on a condom and ground himself into her, scraping her back and shoulders against the wall in his eagerness. She didn't mind. She cared only for him as he rode her fast and hard. Arching her pelvis to meet his thrusts, she cried out. Again, he took her to that strange, wild world that was theirs alone. Clinging to him fiercely, her heart pounded in mad unison with his.

Afterward, their bodies drenched in perspiration, they sank to the floor with their arms still wound around each other.

"I don't know if I can ever stand up again," Summer whispered breathlessly.

"Not to worry, sweetheart. You don't have to."

He lifted her and carried her through the house to the bed in the room she'd used that first weekend. Then he lay down beside her and stared at her hot, damp body gleaming in the moonlight.

When she was with him like this, she felt almost sick with

pleasure and terror of losing him. She thought about her secret and how he might react when she confided in him. How, when could she tell him?

The long, lonely years without him had taught her what loss felt like, and she dreaded anything coming between them again. But something would. All it might take was her confession about the baby.

She'd been young when she'd loved him before. People like Thurman, who'd been wrong in all the advice they'd given her, had told her she'd been lucky to have lost their baby girl, lucky a lowlife like Zach was out of her life, lucky that she could start over. They'd said she would meet someone else, someone respectable, have another baby, that all would be just fine.

She'd learned better. Thurman had been wrong about almost everything, but he'd been especially wrong about how she felt about losing Zach's baby and about losing Zach himself. Yes, she had her career, and she'd enjoyed national, even international, acclaim. But never once in all those years had she felt this alive.

Zach was special. When she'd been a foolish, naive girl, he'd lived in a shack. He'd been considered beneath her by the kids at school, and she'd still thought he was the one. Until Thurman and his cohorts had twisted and turned their love into something ugly and sordid and had driven them apart.

Now Zach rolled over, took her hand and interlocked his fingers with hers. When he looked at her, her blood beat with a mixture of desire and fear. When she kissed him, she realized she was going to take the easy way out…at least for now. They could talk in the morning. The happiness she felt was simply too precious to risk.

That night they made love several more times, but early Saturday morning, when they might have talked, Zach had to go to the site because his contractor had encountered a new challenge. Then he wanted to see Nick. He said they'd had a minor quarrel earlier in the week and he wanted to make things right on his way home.

"I hope you didn't quarrel about me."

His eyes narrowed, and she knew that they had.

"I see. Okay, then," she agreed, feeling a little relief at the reprieve, deciding it was probably best for him to handle Nick as he saw fit. "You'd better stop by. Last week I was terrible in rehearsals, so I really need to go over the script."

But no sooner was he gone than her whirling emotions centered on her secret and him and she was unable to concentrate. Her need to confess made her as uncertain as a young girl in the throes of first love, and she could do nothing except worry about what Nick might say against her.

Hours passed. Unable to focus, she stared at the daisies and her script.

Her phone rang. When she saw it was Gram, she answered it, glad of the distraction.

"I've got some news. I was calling to invite you and Zach over to dinner. I could tell you then."

"I'll ask Zach…. See what he says." *If they went out to dinner, it would be more difficult to find the perfect moment to confess.*

"Tell Zach I'm cooking chicken and Andouille gumbo, crawfish étoufée and a shrimp salad. Oh, and those chocolate-chip cookies he loves so much. Maybe after dinner we could play Hearts."

When Gram hung up, Summer remained as unfocused as ever, even as she comforted herself that it was all right not to work, that sometimes procrastination was part of any actress's process.

Finally, Zach's car roared into the drive out back. Jumping up, breathing hard, she ran to a tall window where she stood until she saw a reporter. Only with the greatest effort did she tiptoe back to the table, pick up a pen and sit down before her script. But when Zach walked through the front door and called to her, she answered with her next breath.

"In here! Working!" She giggled at that last.

He strode inside the kitchen and kissed her. "Sorry it took so long. I hope you got something done."

"I tried," she said evasively.

Her frustration must have shown because he ran his knuckles up the curve of her neck. "Sounds like somebody needs a holiday."

"Right.... It's your fault I couldn't work. I *was* thinking about you the whole time you were gone."

"Ditto." He swept her into his arms and devoured her mouth in a dizzying kiss.

As eager as he, she tore off her clothes while watching him do the same. They ended up making love on the kitchen table—but only after she'd removed the precious daisies for safekeeping.

"Oh," she said, while they were dressing afterward. "I almost forgot and Gram would have killed me...."

"What?"

"She said she had something to tell us, and she invited us over for dinner tonight."

"It must be nice, having family to share things with," he said.

She realized it was, even if Gram had her own ideas about how Summer's life should be and never stopped pushing for her own agenda.

"I take it that's a yes," she said.

Zach would never know exactly at what point that night he knew for sure that no matter what she'd done in the past, no matter what the masses believed, Summer was the one woman who was essential to his happiness. Nothing spectacular happened; it was simply a very special evening.

To elude the paparazzi, he had a pair of doubles drive away in his Mercedes so he and Summer could slip out the back to the dock and take his airboat. As they sped along the glassy water, laughing like children, the sun glowed like gold in the cypress trees, turning the bayou into a gilded ribbon of flashing darkness and light.

Summer's hair whipped back from her pale face, and her heavily lashed blue eyes shone every time she glanced at him as if she were as exhilarated by his nearness as he was by hers. She wore a navy dress with tiny white buttons and held the filmy skirt down with hands pressed against her knees.

Why had he thought he couldn't get beyond their past and her fame? Despite the betrayals, when they were together, he forgave her everything and felt as comfortable around her as he had as a kid. Upon reaching Viola's rambling old plantation house, he followed Summer around the yard as she stooped in the tall grasses to pick wild violets for the dinner table while amusing him with tales about her funniest roles. In turn, he talked about all the various disasters that could befall a construction project.

"I can't believe a giant crane costing millions can actually topple over," she said, sounding amazed.

"Yes, we were so lucky nobody was killed, we didn't even care about the money."

They smiled and laughed together. Holding hands, they carried armfuls of violets into the house, which was redolent with the smell of Cajun spices. Together they looked for a vase and finished setting the table while Tuck followed them around like a lost puppy.

"Tuck's very good at looking like he's doing something when he isn't," Summer whispered when steaming dishes needed to be carried to the table and her brother chose that moment to say he had to go to the bathroom.

"He'll grow up. You'll see."

"We keep hoping...."

Zach enjoyed the simple dinner party. When Viola started tapping her crystal goblet filled with ruby-red wine, Zach felt Summer tense beside him.

"Careful, Gram. Mama's crystal," she chided.

Gram shot her a look. "I'm always careful with dear Anna's crystal. I was only trying to get your attention, dear." She took a deep breath. "And now that you're all listening—I have something to tell you, something I couldn't be more thrilled about." Her sharp blue eyes sparkled like a naughty child's.

"Oh, no, now what have you gone and done?" Summer asked.

In the flattering candlelight and in her soft gray dress with those sharp, mischievous eyes dancing, Viola looked years younger than her age.

"Well, your Gram has bought herself a condo in Plantation Alley."

"Without even telling me," Summer said, shocked.

"I told you I was thinking about it, didn't I? It was such a good deal. I had to snap it up. Besides, you're never here, dear. If you lived closer, maybe I'd form the habit of confiding in you."

"Well, I'm here now," Summer said. "I've been here all weekend."

"I wouldn't dream of disturbing you, child," her grandmother replied innocently, slanting a pointed glance at Zach. "And you didn't drop by...not till I invited you."

"Zing," Summer murmured in Zach's ear.

"Stop whispering, you two! I want to hear everything that's said at my table."

He squeezed Summer's hand.

"Do you want to hear about my new condo or not?" Viola asked peevishly.

"We want to hear," Summer soothed.

Viola brought them a folder that contained a colorful brochure spelling out the amenities of the complex as well as a contract and a copy of the deposit she'd put down. Then she described the condo she'd bought in detail. Several of her friends already lived in the complex, so she'd have lots of company for playing Hearts. The clincher was that Silas approved. He simply adored the cozy window with the view of the bayou where he could sit and watch birds.

"The girls and I sort of thought that if we lived in the same complex we could look after each other, call one another every day, you know."

"The girls are her Friday Lunch Bunch," Summer explained. "They eat together every Friday at a restaurant another friend owns. That's where they hatch their mischief, which mainly has to do with thinking up schemes to meddle in my and Tuck's lives."

"We do not!"

Zach picked up the contract and scratched a few things out, added a sentence or two, explaining why he'd made the changes.

"I'm not sure I understand," Gram said.

"Just take this to Davis first thing Monday. Tell him I sent you. He'll take care of you."

Gram nodded. "It has three bedrooms, so there'll be room for you and Tuck to stay anytime."

"Well, that's a relief. I'm glad you're not kicking me out," Tuck said.

"You won't have to move out on your own, until you're ready, dear. And, Zach, you're always welcome. Silas is so fond of playing Hearts with you."

"Gram! I'm sure Zach's had enough of Silas's opinions for one evening," Summer teased.

"Well, who's going to speak for him, since dear Silas won't speak for himself?"

"Exactly," Summer said.

Tuck hadn't said much during dinner, but he'd come to the table with his hair combed and had answered all Zach's questions about his classes. The small changes in him pleased everyone since he was mildly enthusiastic for a change.

The gumbo and spicy étoufée were delicious.

All in all, it was one of those rare, pleasant evenings, a family evening, the kind of evening Zach hadn't experienced since his Uncle Zach's death. He felt like he belonged—with Summer, with all of them. Suddenly, the past and its pain didn't matter quite so much.

Suddenly, he wanted nothing more than to start over with Summer.

Realizing that thanks to Tuck's misbehavior, they had already started over, Zach took Summer's hand, turned it over in his own, drew it to his lips. For a second he caught a haunted expression in her eyes, but when she flashed him a dazzling smile, he forgot where he was. He would have planted a quick kiss on her cheek if he hadn't caught a very pleased Gram watching his every move. Not in the habit of public displays of affection, he let go of Summer's hand in the next instant.

When dinner was over, they retired to the card table where Gram's three guests conspired to let her win more than her fair share of the games.

"It was a perfect evening," Gram said after they'd helped her clear the table. As they stepped out onto the porch, the black, misty darkness was filled with the cloying scent of honeysuckle and the glorious roar of cicadas. They were saying their goodbyes, and Summer's beautiful face was aglow beneath the porch light.

He loved her, Zach realized.

Love. He hated the word. He'd sworn never to fall under its dark power again, but here he was, lost in its grip. After everything she'd put him through, it was stupid of him, terrifying for him, but he wanted to claim her—to marry her.

When her beaming grandmother read the emotion in his eyes, she closed the door and wisely left them alone. Like a fool, the minute they were alone, he wanted to get down on bended knee in the damp St. Augustine grass and propose.

Luckily, he caught himself, opting to proceed with caution. If this new relationship with Summer was to work, he'd need to reorganize his business, his entire life. He'd need an office in Manhattan for starters. That was okay. He'd worked all over the world; he could work anywhere.

He would have his people contact several knowledgeable Realtors in Manhattan. He'd tell them he wanted to shift the focus of Torr Enterprises, that they were to start searching for opportunities in the northeast. He'd buy Summer a penthouse with a view of Central Park.

Not that he would want to live there all year. But surely she'd meet him halfway by living in Houston or even Louisiana for at least part of the year.

As they sped home across the black, glassy waters of the bayou, Zach seemed quieter, more withdrawn, and yet content.

Their speed wasn't as fast as it had been earlier, since it was dark now and there were patches of ground fog, but there was no way she could speak to him over the roar of the airboat.

Arriving home without incident, she watched as Zach secured the boat quickly and efficiently with the easy expertise of a man who knew exactly what he was doing. Nick had taught him all of that, she thought.

Then Zach pulled her close, and they walked across the lawn holding hands in the moonlight with no paparazzi to spoil the exquisite, shared moment.

He paused beneath the long shadows of the live oak trees to kiss her. She thought his kisses were different somehow, sweeter, and they filled her heart with joy.

Everything felt so right, so perfect—the way it had felt when they'd first fallen in love. It was as if they'd reclaimed their lost innocence and faith in one another. For the first time in years, it was easy to imagine them belonging to each other forever. A knot formed in her throat as she thought about the little girl she'd lost. She had to tell him. But when?

For Summer the evening had been magic. It had been nice to bring Zach to Gram's, so nice to share this man she cared about with her family, especially since her controlling stepfather used to force her to sneak out to see him.

Summer had learned not to stand up to Thurman. It had seemed smarter to maneuver around him. Still, she'd felt like a spineless wimp not taking up for Zach. But if she had, Thurman would have gone ballistic. He would have stopped at nothing to destroy her relationship with Zach.

The only reason Zach had stayed in Bonne Terre that year after his graduation was to wait for her.

Her memories merged with her present need to find a way to tell him about the baby. But when he pulled her close and slanted his hard mouth over hers beneath the shadows of the oak, she sighed and wrapped her hands around his neck to better enjoy the kiss.

Time stopped. There was nothing but the two of them. Their bodies locked as they surrendered to each other in the magical pine-scented darkness. There was no Thurman to stop them now.

She could have kissed him forever, but she began to feel him, hard and swollen, pressing against her thighs. She opened her eyes and met the burning urgency of his gaze.

When he spoke, his voice was rough. "Let's get the hell inside."

Quickly, he took her hand and they ran to the back entrance. When they were in the house, and he'd locked the door, he kissed her again even more fiercely than before. Then he lifted her into his arms and carried her up the stairs into the enveloping darkness of his bedroom.

"Now, where were we, sweetheart?" Zach demanded as he set her on his bed. His eyes were intense as he began to undo the tiny white buttons on her dress.

"I can't believe you want to make love to me after a big old dinner like that."

"Well, I do. We played cards for an hour, didn't we? Besides, do you have a better idea?"

"We could sit outside on the upstairs veranda, enjoy the moonlight and talk...maybe about the past." *About our baby....*

"The past...." He frowned. "I'm in much too good a mood to want to go there. Trust me. We're better off making love, enjoying what we have now. We deserve some happiness."

"But aren't we hiding from things we need to think about and resolve?"

"You expect me to care about what's over and done with, when you're so damn beautiful I hurt?"

But she felt so close to him right now, close enough to tell him everything.... Even tell him about the baby. It would take more than a single conversation, she knew. But she felt a profound need to share everything with him. He had to know the worst.

She wanted him to listen, to hold her, to forgive her, to

grieve with her and then to make love to her. Had she been wrong about their special bond tonight?

He grazed her lips with his mouth with such infinite tenderness he soon sparked a wild conflagration.

But he was a man, and he was aroused. So, now wasn't the time to talk after all.

They could not get their clothes off fast enough. Then they took their time exploring each other. He took his turn kissing and touching her, and then she broke away and started kissing him everywhere, her tongue running down his body until she found his manhood, which was thick and engorged.

She took him into her mouth. He was too close to the edge to endure this for long. Soon he moved on top of her and slid inside.

That was all it took for her to explode.

He thrust deeply and then shuddered, too.

Afterward, as they lay in the darkness, while he held her close, she gathered her courage again. "Wouldn't you feel better if you knew exactly what happened to me and why I might have failed you years ago?"

"What?"

Perspiration glistened on his brow as he rolled over to brush his hand through her tangled hair. "I can't believe you're bringing that up again. Now."

"I just think we should talk. It's a perfect time, after our lovely evening."

"No. Let's not tarnish tonight."

He sat up so he could stare down at her. "Look, I'm not blaming you for the past any longer, if that's why you want to talk about it. On Viola's porch that first day we reconnected, I felt this terrible lingering sadness in you. It made it impossible for me to continue blaming you for everything. That's all the explanation I need about the past. I hurt you, too. I know that."

"But…"

"It's over. I'm trying to forget it. I suggest you do the same."

"But there's something I really need to share…."

He ran a finger around the edges of her lips and shushed her. "Don't ruin what we have right now. It's too special. I want to hold on to it. We can talk later. I promise."

When she frowned, he pulled her close and kissed her.

But he was so adamant, and she wanted this time with him so much, she let him have his way. So, when she left on Sunday, she still hadn't told him about what happened in New Orleans.

"Why don't I come see you next weekend, for a change?" he said as he put her on his jet. "It just so happens I have a few things to do in New York."

"That would be wonderful."

"I'll come up on Thursday, rent a suite at the Pierre and take you anywhere you want to go."

"So, you intend to spoil me hopelessly?"

"Absolutely."

"Lucky me."

"No. Lucky me," he said as he kissed her.

# Ten

Something was different about Zach, and Summer wasn't sure what it was.

Their first three-day weekend together in New York was not as intimate as their previous weekends in Bonne Terre. But that was to be expected under the circumstances. He had business affairs to attend to and she the theater. Only at night could they make time to be together.

If his purpose in coming to the city had been to impress her with his grand lifestyle, he succeeded. His gilded suite was spectacular. Limos followed by the paparazzi whisked them to fabulous dinners and nightclubs where he knew people, some of them beautiful women.

"Zach has a thing for blondes," Roberto, one of his top executives, whispered in her ear while Zach conversed with a beautiful woman during a business dinner.

"Good thing I'm a blonde, then," she quipped.

For the first time since their reunion, Zach hadn't shared

details about his current project. She wondered exactly what he'd done all day while she'd rehearsed. When they were alone later, she grilled him.

"Where were you all afternoon? What business exactly do you have to do here?"

"I'm tweaking an important project."

"Tweaking?"

"I'll explain everything when it's all in order."

"Does this project concern me?"

"I said I'll explain later."

"You're not bored with me and chasing another woman already? Another blonde?"

"Good Lord, no! Whatever gave you that idea?"

She refrained from throwing Roberto to the wolves for one ill-advised remark. "Oh…nothing. Forget I asked."

"There's no other woman for me, and there never will be."

"You're a billionaire. You could have anybody."

"Strange as this may sound, that's not true. Believe me, I have had plenty of time to discover that there's no substitute for the real thing. You're the real thing."

Something twisted near her heart. "Oh. Am I? Tell me more…."

But that was all she could get out of him other than a quick kiss on the tip of her nose.

He was hiding something. *Just as she was.*


The next weekend as Zach stood in a glamorous penthouse that had seventeen gloriously imagined rooms with high ceilings and tall windows, he thought of Summer's cozy apartment. Was the penthouse too much? Would she like it? Women could be very particular about their homes. Maybe he should show it to her before he bought it, but he was too impatient.

She could call the marble and gold vulgar and rip it out if

she didn't like it, he decided. She was too creative not to find a way to make it hers. The location was too stupendous to pass on, and he needed a place like this to impress the business people he dealt with.

All week Zach had been in a fever to ask her to marry him. Every time they'd talked, the question had been at the forefront of his mind. The pressure to wait until he had the ring selected and the penthouse bought and his new offices acquired and a contractor to remodel Thibodeaux House was making him feel explosive.

She'd looked so haunted when she'd tried to talk to him about the past. Was he rushing into this because he knew he should wait?

What if she said no?

Zach opened a glass door and walked out onto the terrace. The air was cool and crisp. Central Park was ablaze with riotous fall colors forty stories beneath him.

"I told you the penthouse was fabulous and the view lovely," the Realtor gushed behind him. "Now do you believe me?"

"I had to make sure," Zach said. "It's a deal, then." He turned and shook the woman's perfectly manicured hand. "Send me a contract."

She grinned brilliantly. "I like you so much."

"Roberto Gomez will be handling this for me."

"Yes. I've already had several emails from him. Charming man. It's been a pleasure...."

Zach nodded, turned on his heel and strode toward the elevator. He had a long day ahead of him and no time to waste.

He'd arrived in Manhattan a day early this weekend to approve his future office space in Lower Manhattan and the penthouse that his most trusted people had selected. Summer didn't expect him until tomorrow.

He was staying at the Pierre. She'd liked the suite there so much last weekend, he'd rented it again.

In the elevator, he slipped his hand into his pocket and touched the small, black-velvet box.

Tomorrow, at the Pierre, when they were alone, he would offer her a glass of champagne, get down on his knee and hand it to her.

When he got off at the bottom floor, his excitement about the gorgeous penthouse and his new offices and the ring was so great he wanted to share his news with her. Why wait until tomorrow to propose when he felt so sure this afternoon?

Why not go to the theater and propose to her now? He knew she was in rehearsals and that they hadn't been going well. He knew he shouldn't bother her. Still, he wanted to see her. He wanted to hold her. Most of all he felt an urgent need to propose to her. He was afraid if he waited, somehow he'd lose her again.

He pulled out his phone and studied his calendar. Calling Roberto, he told him to cancel the rest of his meetings.

Then he stepped into his limo and ordered his driver to take him to her theater.

Bad idea, he thought. But he couldn't stop himself.

Summer raced to her dressing room during a break in rehearsals to return her agent's calls, of which there were three. She hoped the call wouldn't take long because she wanted so badly to call Zach.

Carl answered on the first ring. "You're an angel for getting back to me so fast."

"What is it?"

"Hugh Jones is in town. Just for the day. The PR people from the studio want to set up a short interview for the two of you."

"When? Where? I'm really busy."

"They had a hard time talking Jones into it as well, but they've got him to agree. So—say in an hour. In your dressing room."

"Impossible. Things for the show aren't going well, and some of the production's big investors are here giving Paolo a hard time. He's pretty insane."

"The studio has already talked to Paolo. He's fine with it."

"What?"

"The interview won't take more than fifteen minutes. There was so much buzz about your scenes with Jones that…"

She shut her eyes. That buzz, as Carl termed it, had nearly destroyed her relationship with Zach. Except for the fact that she hadn't found a way to tell him about the baby, things were going so well for them right now. She didn't want to stir up another round of press interest, and Hugh was a hot button she didn't want punched until Zach truly trusted her and their relationship was on less fragile ground. Until she'd told him about the baby….

"The movie isn't coming out for months. I don't see why I have to do an interview with Hugh this afternoon."

"Well, the PR department makes those calls, not us. Their team thinks it's essential to keep up the momentum."

Translation: they wanted hordes of paparazzi questioning the true nature of her relationship with Jones and continuing to chase her and take pictures of her with Zach. The PR department wanted her face and name out there, so she'd be a draw. They didn't care that by linking her to Jones, they drove Zach crazy. To them, this was just another juicy story.

She had to protect her relationship with Zach at all costs.

"Sorry!" she said and ended the call. But no sooner had she hung up than Sam rang her.

"You signed a contract agreeing to do promotion. Paolo's okay with it, so what's your problem?" Sam read her the clause in her contract. It didn't take a genius to understand his thinly veiled threat. They could sue her if she didn't do as they commanded.

Feeling queasy and a bit shaky, which had been happening a lot lately, especially in the mornings, she hung up and called Zach's cell.

But his phone went to voice mail. She didn't want to leave this kind of news in a message. When she called him repeatedly, and he still didn't answer, she began to feel sick with worry. She had to tell him about this interview before the paparazzi caught up with him  and peppered him with questions he was not prepared to answer.

On the way to the theater Zach's limo got caught in traffic beside a flower stall, so Zach whipped out and bought two dozen roses from the elderly flower seller. The perfect buds were so bright in the sunlight they blazed like flames, but they burned no brighter than the towering emotion in his heart.

Inside the limo, their scent was so overpowering he set them aside. When the driver braked, Zach leaned forward, staring at the sea of vehicles surrounding them, cursing vividly when a truck cut in front of them.

Damn it. He sat back against soft leather and forced himself to try to relax. But he couldn't. He was out of control, which he hated. He was impatient to see Summer, to take her in his arms and beg her to love him. To ask her to make a life with him.

He could walk iron without breaking a sweat. So what was so terrifying about baring his soul and asking the woman he loved to marry him?

When his cell phone rang, Zach answered it automatically.

"You bastard!"

"Hello, Thurman."

Zach hadn't heard the other man's voice in years. Funny, that he recognized the cold, dead tone instantly.

"You think you're so smart, that you know everything, but you don't. You're a gambler. I'd bet money Summer hasn't told you what she did in New Orleans...."

The hair at the back his nape rose. "What the hell are you talking about?"

"Why don't you ask Summer?"

Thurman laughed nastily and hung up.

When Zach jumped out of the limo at the theater with a conflicted heart, a dozen reporters leaped toward him, hammering him about Summer as their flashes blinded him.

His expression turned to stone as he stormed past them into the auditorium, slamming the door on their idiotic clamor.

Zach was remembering how vulnerable Summer had looked every time she'd tried to talk to him about the past. What hadn't she told him? What did Thurman know that Zach didn't?

He knew exactly where Summer's dressing room was since she'd given him a personal tour last weekend, so he wasted no time on his way through the crowded corridors. Backstage was like a maze, but he didn't stop, not even when actors, who were milling about, tried to greet him.

He wondered why everyone was on break. Maybe this meant Summer would be free to talk to him. He wouldn't have to wait.

When he found the door with her name on it, it was closed. He banged on it impatiently.

What he wanted was beautiful golden Summer with her long-lashed eyes to open the door and blush charmingly when she saw him. He wanted to take her in his arms and then set a time for a private talk. This time he would listen to whatever she had to tell him. Then he would tell her how much he loved her and ask her to be his wife.

What he got was Hugh Jones and a photographer.

The reporter didn't miss a beat when he saw the chance for a shot of the two men together.

When the flash went off twice, Zach turned on his heel. No way could he face the press when he felt so conflicted privately. Then Summer was behind him, her voice nervous and high-pitched.

Instead of smiling, her blue eyes were wide with panic and guilt. "Zach, what are you doing here?"

Logically, he knew he shouldn't have interrupted her on such short notice, but he wasn't feeling logical.

"Making a damn fool of myself. Again."

"Zach, no.... Wait! Listen!"

She'd gone pale, and her hand shook as it tugged at his sleeve. He felt sorry for her, so he let her pull him into the dressing room beside hers and listened impatiently as she whispered to the young actress inside it. "Can we please talk here for a few minutes?"

"Sure. Anytime." Moving like a dancer, the girl, who was thin as a rail, got up languidly, picked up the magazine she'd been flipping through and left in a swirl of silken yellow skirts as she winked at Zach.

"We were just doing an interview for *Dangerous Man*. That's all. My agent called me less than an hour ago or I would have told you.... I had to do it. Because I signed a contract saying I would. I tried to call you, but you didn't answer."

"I understand. I was on the phone." *With Thurman,* he thought, frowning.

"No, you don't understand. I can see that. You look furious...."

"I said I believe you're doing an interview, and I do. But before the press is through with this story, nobody else will. I can't help wondering if this will always be the way we have to live—with the press playing up your nonexistent relationships with other men and making me look the fool."

He knew he wasn't being totally honest. He felt too raw to be completely open with her. He'd come here to propose, and then Thurman had called and stirred up all his old doubts about her.

"Zach, I want you in my life. I do…. What are you doing here a day early?"

He shouldn't have surprised her like this. He felt vulnerable, as if his heart was on his sleeve, and suddenly he didn't want her to know about all the plans he'd made. Now wasn't the time to ask her about New Orleans or to propose.

"It doesn't matter. I'm leaving."

"I wish you'd stay."

"Well, I'm not sure I want idiots second-guessing every stage of our relationship when I feel…" He stopped, torn.

"When you feel…what?"

"Nothing."

"Zach, what's wrong?"

"Maybe I'm not in the mood to share you with everyone in the known universe. So, I'd better go, so you can finish the damn interview. The entire crew and cast is waiting on you, right?"

She swallowed. "Talk to me, Zach. Please talk to me."

Her eyes were so earnest maybe he would have, if a red-faced Paolo hadn't burst into the room, shattering the moment.

"Sorry to interrupt, but Sandy said you were in here. You did say fifteen minutes. How much longer is this damn interview going to take?"

"Sorry. We haven't started yet."

"Why the hell not?"

"It's my fault, but I'm going," Zach said.

"No!" she cried, grabbing him.

Paolo shot him a look of disgust before he turned and left.

"I'm beginning to realize how demanding I am," Zach said. "You see, I'm the kind of guy who expects his wife to put him first sometimes…like now, even when I know it's a very bad time for you."

"Your wife…. Did you say *your wife?*"

"I came over here because I had something very personal to say to you…. Something very important, to me at least. Now I see that you have a lot more to deal with than my concerns."

"Zach, did you come over here to ask me to marry you? Because I will."

He didn't want to ask her now, like this. He was beginning to think he shouldn't ask her at all. Instead of answering her, he said, "On the way over here I got a phone call. From Thurman."

"Thurman?" She went very white.

"He told me to ask you about New Orleans. He insinuated that you've been keeping something important from me. Is that true?"

"Oh, Zach…." Her eyes misted with guilt-stricken anguish. Her hands were shaking. "I…I tried to tell you in Louisiana. I want to talk about it. Truly I do, but not now. I have rehearsals, the interview…and you're too upset."

"It doesn't matter," he said.

He saw now that he'd been a stupid, emotional fool to be in such a rush to marry her. They both had huge, time-consuming careers; their past had haunted them for years; the press wouldn't leave them alone. Was there room for love and marriage with so many distractions, responsibilities and conflicts?

"Maybe neither of us has time for a marriage," he said.

"That's not fair. This is just a very bad time for me. What if I happened to drop in on you, when you were in the middle of a negotiation and forty people were waiting on your decision?"

"That's the point, isn't it? I've just realized there's not room in a marriage for two huge egos and two big careers…along with everything else that's between us. I don't like goodbyes, Summer, so I'll just make a quick exit."

"You're not telling me everything," she said, grabbing his arm to keep him in the room.

"I could say the same thing to you, couldn't I, sweetheart?"

The last thing he saw was her ashen face as she staggered backward, knocking a wig stand over as she sank down onto her friend's couch. Her big blue eyes glimmered with unshed tears, and she looked white and shaken. It tore him up to realize he'd hurt her again.

But maybe there had always been too much between them for a relationship to ever work. Maybe he'd let their chemistry blind him. Had he been rushing into marriage because he hadn't wanted to stop to think about the realities?

On his way out of the theater, he pitched the perfect red roses in the first stinking trash barrel he saw. Then he stepped through the throng of reporters and into the hushed silence of his luxurious limo.

"Take me to LaGuardia Airport," he said.

# Eleven

**Summer Wallace Dumps Billionaire For Movie Star.**

Summer felt sick to her stomach as she sat up straighter in her bed to turn the page of the newspaper.

She'd tried to phone Zach, but he wouldn't take her calls. She had to tell him about their lost little girl even if the timing was awful and the news killed whatever remaining tenderness he felt for her.

*"When will the thirty-one-year-old actress make up her mind...."*

There was an awful picture of Zach and Hugh together. Two more shots showed Zach entering the theater with roses, and there was one of him looking furious as he dumped the gorgeous bouquet on his way out.

Why did the headlines always have to mention her age and remind her that her biological clock was ticking? Why did every headline have to remind her that Zach would never marry her? That she would never have his darling black-haired children.

She felt a rivulet of perspiration trickle down her back. Then a hot sensation of dizziness flooded her. Cupping her hands over her mouth, she lurched to her feet and ran to her toilet where she was violently ill.

When she was able to lift her head, she opened the window and gulped in mouthfuls of sweet, fresh air. Then she put the toilet lid down and sat, holding her head in her hands.

The episode of nausea was the third she'd had this week. Since her stomach was often queasy during rehearsals and she'd been so busy, she hadn't really thought about it. Until now.

"Oh, no," she whispered as comprehension dawned.

Slowly she arose and stared critically at the reflection of her white face in the mirror.

She was pregnant. Since she'd been pregnant before, she should have recognized the signs. Her breasts were swollen, and her period was late. She had the oddest cravings at the strangest times. Like that other night when she had to have a corn dog and a tomato and a pickle and nothing else would do. She felt lethargic, different.

Great timing. Just like last time.

Zach had left her. And she hadn't even told him about their little girl yet. He wouldn't be happy to learn the truth about their past, nor would he be overjoyed that they were going to have another child.

Then there was the not-insignificant detail that she was starring in a play that was going to open in less than three weeks. One where her character was not pregnant and the director and cast were on the verge of a collective nervous breakdown if things didn't start coming together soon.

Zach had been swimming laps in his pool behind Thibodeaux House for an hour, so it was time to get out.

He wanted to forget Summer, to go on with his life. So, he'd ignored her calls; ignored the pain he felt at her loss.

He would get through this. He would. Not that it would be easy.

As he toweled off, he heard furious shouts and scuffling out front.

At first he thought it was the press and paid no attention. They'd been stalking him all week, ever since they'd caught him with Jones the day of the interview. Then he recognized the hateful voice.

"Let me through, damn it," Thurman Wallace yelled at Zach's security team. "I've got something to say to Torr, and I won't go until I say it."

Pulling on a shirt without bothering to button it, Zach strode to the front of the house. "Let him in," he said.

When Wallace stepped through the gate, Zach smelled the hot stench of liquor on the man's breath.

"Say your piece and leave, Wallace."

"You think you're something, don't you, you arrogant you-know-what, coming back here, to my town, getting everyone on your side because you're rich…. Taking up with Summer again…. Using her like a…"

"Watch your language. Say your piece. Then get the hell off my property."

"It wasn't all me, wanting to bring those charges. You think she wanted you back then, but she didn't. She thought you were trash, same as I did."

"Shut up about her."

"If she'd cared for you, why did she kill your baby?"

"What the hell did you say?"

"You got her pregnant. I had to send her to New Orleans before she started to show so nobody around here would know about her and ruin my good name."

"I don't believe you! Get out of here before I throw you out!"

When Wallace didn't move, Zach started toward him. "Get out of here now, or you'll be sorry!"

Wallace took one look at Zach and ran for his life.

Zach sank to his knees and thought about a younger Summer, pregnant and alone in New Orleans. Whatever she'd done, he'd never believe she'd deliberately killed their baby. But she hadn't told him about it, had she? So, how could he trust her?

All doubt that he had made the right decision in leaving her vanished.

The sudden certainty hurt.

God, how it hurt.

### Billionaire And Actress Had Secret Baby!

The ugly headline screamed at Summer, shattering her heart into a million tiny pieces.

Gram had warned her about the awful story that Thurman had sold to the tabloids. In spite of the warning, Summer was still shaking as she laid down a wad of cash for all the newspapers on the rack at the tiny grocery store a block from her apartment.

Folding them, she plunged them into her bag, put her sunglasses back on and ran outside where she dumped them in the first trash bin she saw. It was a hollow gesture since there were hundreds of thousands on similar racks all over the country. Everybody would see them when they were in the check-out lines.

How could Thurman be so filled with hate? How could he have sold such a personally heartbreaking story? She felt brokenhearted, betrayed and mortified at the same time. But most of all she hurt for Zach. This was no way for him to discover the truth.

Until now, she'd held on to a fragile hope that Zach might be missing her as much as she missed him, and that given time, he would change his mind and come back to her.

Thurman's story extinguished all such hope.

She felt like weeping, not just for herself, but for the baby she was carrying.

Then a reporter sprang out of nowhere and called her name. When she turned, he took her picture.

"Gram, I've got to talk to Zach."

A week had passed since Thurman's story had hit the stands. Zach was still refusing to take her calls. His secretary was impatient whenever Summer called his office and left a message. So she'd called Gram, hoping for her help.

"But I thought that he and you...that it was...over," Gram said.

"It is," Summer said softly. "I've called him so many times, and he won't talk to me. But that's not the worst. Gram, I'm pregnant. I don't know how it happened...because we were always careful."

"It was meant to be," Gram said in her know-it-all way.

"No," Summer replied, knowing Gram couldn't be right. "What this means is that in spite of everything that's wrong between us, I've got to talk to him."

"Nick told Moxie Brown, who told Sammy, who told me that Zach has fired the contractor he'd hired to remodel that old Thibodeaux place and has put it up for sale. Nick said that big gambling boat of his is arriving at the end of the week. So, Zach's coming to town to inspect it."

Summer let out a breath. Finally, she'd caught a break. Once the play opened, she'd be doing eight shows a week. It would be very difficult for her to take time off. Paolo would pitch a fit, but maybe she could sneak in an overnight trip home.

She couldn't make the same mistake she'd made the first time they'd broken up, when he'd put up roadblocks and she'd given up on telling Zach the truth about their little girl.

She had to see him one last time—to tell him face-to-face about the baby they'd lost and this precious baby that she was carrying.

Their baby.

Summer barely glanced at the chain-link fence covered with No Trespassing notices meant to keep out the press. And her. Nor did she take note of the large sign over the gate that blared in big red letters, No Admittance. Employees Only.

Hunched over, with a pink pashmina covering her hair, Summer rushed past a uniformed man.

"Ma'am, you can't go in there. Ma'am…"

Running now on her ice-pick heels, Summer ignored the burly individual in the hard hat and brown uniform as she sped toward the dock where Zach's magnificent floating gambling palace was now secured.

"Ma'am!"

*What luck!* There he was.

Every muscle in her body tensed. Then she forced herself to let out a breath.

Holding a clipboard and pen, Zach stood in the middle of a dozen men. His stance, with long legs spread slightly apart, reminded her of a large cat who looked relaxed but was coiled to spring. His face was hard, and he was talking fast. The other men, their heads cocked toward him, held clipboards and pens, too. Those standing beside him were frowning in frustration as they wrote furiously in an effort to keep up.

"Zach," she cried, pink heels clattering as she ran farther out onto the dock.

She wore a soft pink dress. The bodice clung and its skirt swirled around her hips. Once he'd accused her of dressing to be desirable. Well, today she'd given it her best shot. She'd gone shopping and had deliberately picked a sexy dress for this confrontation.

All the men stopped talking at once. She let her pashmina slide to her shoulders.

Jaws fell. Zach spun, then hissed in a breath at the sight of her. Even though his eyes went icy and hard, she'd seen the split-second spark of attraction her appearance had caused. She'd caught him off guard in front of his men, exposed his vulnerability, and she knew he hated that.

Grief that he was hers no longer, that she couldn't run into his arms, slashed through her like a knife.

He didn't look as sure or confident as he had the last time she'd seen him. His face was thinner; his eyes shadowed.

"Get her out of here," he ordered, his frigid voice radiating antagonism.

"Sorry, Mr. Torr. Ma'am, I'm gonna have to ask you to leave," the burly man said behind her.

She had only seconds before she'd be forced to go.

"Zach," she cried. "I've got to talk to you."

"Too bad. I'm in a meeting." Slamming on a pair of dark glasses, he turned away.

The burly man grabbed her arm and began to tug her gently in the direction of the exit. "Please, ma'am..."

Frantic, she struggled to free herself. "Zach... You've got to listen to me."

The man's grip hardened. "Come on, ma'am."

*"Zach! Please!"*

His face tight and determined, Zach tapped his pen against his clipboard and continued to ignore her.

She didn't want to tell him like this—not when he was

surrounded by other people. She didn't. But what were her choices?

*"Zach, I'm pregnant!"*

Zach had selected the elegant office onboard his ship as a place where they could be alone, but the space felt cramped and airless to Summer as Zach subjected her to a thorough, intimate appraisal. Never had she found his arresting face more handsome, but when she searched its hard, angular planes for a trace of sympathy, she found none.

His eyes were so intense and cold, they made her feel almost faint with grief.

"Zach…" For a second, everything in her vision darkened except his face, which blurred in swirling pinpricks of light.

His hard arms reached for her, steadied her, led her to a chair, where she gulped in a sweet breath of air.

"Are you okay?" he demanded.

"I—I'm fine."

He stood over her, watching her carefully to make sure.

"Zach, I didn't want to tell you the news like that…in front of your men…when you were so furious. But I had to tell you face-to-face. I didn't want to leave a message with your secretary, or for some reporter to accost you with questions because I was having our child."

"Oh, really? You didn't bother to tell me the last time you were pregnant. Are you eager to share this child with me since I've got money now? And when do you intend to tell the press, so as to heighten your box-office draw? Frankly, I'm surprised you didn't bring the hounds with you today."

Again Zach's eyes had become emotionless. She felt as if her heart were freezing and dying. It was as if, instead of her, he saw some cruel, cunning stranger.

She took a deep breath. "No… Why would I… You can't, you can't believe I'm that low."

"You're wrong."

"I want to protect our baby. And I have my own income, I'll have you know. So, money is the last thing I need from you."

"I'll set up an account and do what's necessary. But the less I see or hear from you, the better. In the future, my lawyers will talk to your lawyers. I'll want to see our child rather frequently, I'm afraid. As you know, I'm sorely lacking in close family. And as I distrust the mother, I'll need to be as big an influence in his life as possible if he's to have a fighting chance. And I repeat, I will see to it that these matters are arranged so that we meet as infrequently as possible."

"I—I know how you must feel...finding out the way you did...about our first baby. You must think me truly awful...."

"No! You don't know how I feel! You couldn't possibly imagine."

For a moment his hard face was expressionless. Then he shook his head. "You don't understand me at all."

"I know I didn't stand up for you the way you wanted me to when my stepfather brought charges against you. You thought I went along with him, but I didn't. I loved you. I still do."

"Don't use that four-letter word. You say it too easily. All it's ever been for me is a one-way ticket to hell."

"Zach, I was sixteen...pregnant...terrified...of him and of the accusations, of all the ugliness. I was so confused. Hysterical, really."

"It doesn't matter anymore," he said in a weary, defeated tone.

But it did matter to her, fiercely. She'd thought she'd learned to live with her regrets, then he'd come back into her life and made her love him again. Being with him right now, when he was so distant, knowing that he was shutting her out forever, made her want to confess everything, to finally share all the regrets she'd carried alone for so long.

She'd organized a funeral for their first baby, had attended it by herself in the rain. Her mother, who would have come, had been too ill to leave Bonne Terre. Gram had been caring for Summer's mother, and Tuck had been too young to be of any comfort. Summer had stayed in the cemetery until she'd been drenched, until the last clod of dirt had been thrown, until a compassionate grave digger had plucked a single white rose from the funeral wreath she'd bought and handed the dripping blossom to her.

"Press this in that Bible you be carrin', *cher*. And go home. You can't do any good here. The little one, she's in heaven now."

Summer had placed angels on the grave.

Somehow she swallowed her tears when she came back to the present. "I went to Houston when I was nearly five months along. I tried to talk to you, to find you, but you wouldn't see me."

"Because I knew you were manipulating me."

"But I tried to tell you about the baby. I really tried."

"Not hard enough apparently. You could have told somebody else…. My uncle, maybe. He would have gotten the message to me. But you didn't."

"I was out of money. I wasn't feeling so well. I—I thought it was no use, so I went back to New Orleans. I—I lost the baby the next week. I was all alone. I wanted you so desperately. I never wanted you with me more."

A muscle in his carved cheek jerked savagely, but when he spoke, his voice was low, contemptuous.

"You didn't do anything deliberate to bring about that unhappy event, did you?"

"What?" His words hit her like a blow. Once again his face swirled in blackness. If she'd been standing, she would have fallen. Only with the greatest effort did she manage to catch her breath.

"No." The single word was a prayer asking him to be-lieve her. The single tear that traced down her cheek spoke the truth.

Not that he could see the truth, blinded as he was by his own fury and sense of betrayal.

"You damn sure know how to deliver a line." His low voice was hoarse. "I'll give you that. You need to remember that little trick for the stage, sweetheart. It was very effective."

"Okay. I understand," she whispered. "You'll never trust me again. Or forgive me."

"You've got that right. The sooner we finish this conversa-tion, the sooner we can get on with our separate lives. I said I'd help you with the baby, and I will. You don't look well. I want you to take better care of yourself this time. Cut back on your schedule. You can't possibly do eight shows a week. I'll pay for the best doctors…anything you need. And I want to be there when you deliver. Not for your sake, but for the baby's."

She nodded, feeling crushed at his efficient tone.

"I love you," she murmured. "I'll always love you."

"Then I'm sorry for you because it's over between us. I consider myself a stupid fool for getting involved with you again. Usually I'm smart enough to learn from my mistakes. Nick tried to warn me you were nuclear. He was right."

"I'm so sorry I've caused you so much pain…."

"Sorry never cuts it, does it?"

Ravaged, she stood up. Then turning from him, she fled.

Outside, the sunlight in the trees was as dull as old pewter, and she was deaf to her favorite song playing on her car radio.

She didn't want to go back to New York and work on-stage, work with people. She wanted to curl up somewhere in a dark room and cry.

Then she remembered Gram's tin of chocolate-chip cook-ies on the shelf above her fridge. She would go back to Gram's and confide in her. Her grandmother would take Summer in her arms as she had after Summer had lost Zach, her mother and her little baby girl, and, for a brief spell, she'd feel better. Then she'd stuff herself on her grandmother's cookies until she fell asleep.

Slowly, she'd gather enough courage to go through the motions of living. She'd pack her suitcase and set her alarm. Tomorrow she'd dress and drive to the airport. Then she'd return to her lonely apartment and get back in her old routine and try to forget Zach all over again.

It wouldn't be possible, but she'd try just the same.

The memory of her soft, pale face with those unshed tears tore at him.

"I can't do this. Take over for me," Zach growled as he slammed his clipboard down on a table inside the casino.

Roberto and his men watched silently as Zach stalked past them, the rows of slot machines and then the gaming tables. Outside, the air was thick and oppressive with the scent of rain. He looked up and saw threatening black clouds moving in fast. A fierce gust ripped across the bayou.

*Perfect weather,* he thought, as the first raindrop pelted him.

No sooner had he slammed the door of his Mercedes, started the engine and roared out of the parking lot, than it started pouring. Not that the rain kept him from whipping violently across the narrow bridge and skidding onto the main road. A truck honked wildly. Brakes squealed as it surrendered right-of-way.

Zach took his foot off the accelerator. No use killing some innocent motorist. Summer damn sure wasn't worth it.

It was going to take a long time for his love, or rather the illusion of who he'd believed she was, to die again.

*Maybe forever.*

She'd looked so damn pretty in that soft pink dress that

had clung to her slim body, and so desperately forlorn with those damp blue eyes that had shed that single spectacular tear at exactly the right moment. She'd shredded his heart all over again. It would probably thrill her to know she'd nearly had him believing what he saw and felt instead of what he knew to be true.

His gut had clenched, and his heart had thudded violently. He'd wanted to grab her, pull her close, soothe and console her, kiss that tearstained cheek and those beautiful, pouting lips…just one last time. He'd wanted it so much he'd almost lost control.

Then he'd remembered she was an actress, who'd dressed to entice him, who'd played her role perfectly despite her vows never to act when she was with him.

He remembered all her lies of omission about the baby. What part of their relationship had ever been true? What was he to her? Another circus act in the three-ring show she put on for her adoring fans? Did she need a man in her life to complete the picture of her as America's number-one sweetheart? Acting was a highly competitive career. What sin wouldn't she commit to stay on top?

He thought of all the magazine-cover stories he'd seen about actresses with their adoring babies and husbands. Were any of those heartwarming stories truthful? Weren't they all just fodder for fools like him, who, deep down, wanted to believe the dream?

Had anything she'd said today been real?

Whether it was or not, she'd damn sure shattered his heart and sent him to hell and back all over again.

# Twelve

*One week later*

Zach moved silently through the long shadows of the tall spreading oaks near Viola's house, stepping past Silas, who looked like a black-and-white fur ball as he napped under the pink blossoms of his favorite crape myrtle bush.

The dazzling pink flowers blurred, and suddenly Zach saw Summer instead of the worthless feline: Summer with her heart in her eyes, Summer looking lovely and too sexy for words in that ridiculous pink confection of a dress.

Damn her. As the image dissolved, he experienced burning, agonizing loss.

Frowning, he approached Viola's screen door warily.

Why was he even here? He had a plane to catch. It wasn't as if he had to show up at her request. Hell, these days he ignored most invitations, and he had every reason to ignore Viola's. Why was he putting himself through this?

*Because she'd sounded so fragile when she'd summoned him. Because he genuinely liked her. Because she was family now, in spite of everything Summer had done. Viola would be his son's great-grandmother. Because she was hurting nearly as much as he was that the dream wouldn't come true.*

Viola's bossy cat trotted toward the screen door and rubbed his tail arrogantly against Zach's jeans. Then he sank a claw into the screen as he waited to be let in.

Viola welcomed them both. Silas, who sprang inside first, she gave a can of tuna. Zach, she gave a plate of chocolate-chip cookies and a glass of iced tea that she'd flavored with mint from her garden.

He didn't have time for tea or cookies, but he was loath to say so. Viola had a strange power over him.

When he saw the empty shelves and all the boxes stacked against the walls in every room, in an effort to make polite conversation, he asked when she planned to move to her new condo.

"I'm taking my time. I can only do an hour or so of packing each day before my back starts howling. Tuck's not much help, bless his lazy soul, not even when I pay him. Slow as molasses. Drops things, he does. And Summer's not going to rent out this old place after all. Because of the baby…." She said that last with reverence as she lifted her sharp gaze to his.

When she didn't avert those piercing eyes that saw too much, his heart sped up to a tortured pace.

"She's feeling quite sentimental about the old place. Said she's going to keep it for herself and the baby, so the baby will grow up loving it as much as past generations have before her. That's nice, don't you think?"

*Her?* Funny how Zach always thought of their kid as a boy. A little boy with golden hair and bright blue eyes. But it could be girl, couldn't it? A beautiful little girl who looked like Summer, who'd break his heart because he loved her so.

Viola noted his empty plate. Usually, she hopped up to refill such a plate. But not today.

"I'm afraid there aren't any more cookies. You see, Summer ate practically all of them the other day…stuffed herself on them, the poor dear. Not a good thing really, in her condition. She has to get into all those costumes, too, you know. But she was so down before she left. Kept eating one after another, couldn't stop herself. Until I took the plate away and froze the remaining cookies for future guests. And here you are."

"Why did you ask me to come over here today, Viola? I have a plane to catch, meetings in Houston…."

"You poor dear, with your big, important life. You know, you don't look any better than she does. I can see that, despite your tough exterior, this is just as hard on you as it is on her."

Zach froze. "Did *she* put you up to this?"

"Who?" Viola's eyes were suspiciously guileless. "Put me up to what?"

Those innocent eyes, so compelling in her wrinkled face, seemed to search his soul in the exact way that Summer's sometimes did. But unlike Summer, Viola's deep compassion for him was genuine.

"Zach, is this really what you want? You two are going to have a child. Summer's brokenhearted, and I think you love her, too. I think you always have and always will."

He felt the ice that encased his heart melting beneath the brightness of her sweet, determined gaze, but his face remained a mask.

"Zach, you have the baby to think of. When parents don't live together, it's the child who suffers most. The family's broken. That's what happened to Summer when her father walked out on Anna. Look at poor Tuck, how he's still struggling. A baby needs to be part of a close, loving family."

"Unfortunately, we can't all have the ideal family," he muttered. "I was on my own after my mother left my father, and then my father remarried a younger woman, who threw me out after he died."

"So, then you know how it feels. Do you want your baby to suffer the way you did, when you could so easily prevent it?"

*Easily?*

Again, he asked himself why he'd come here. It was hard enough to let Summer go without this fragile old lady, whom he liked, trying to pry his innermost secrets from him. Summer was wrong for him. Period.

He'd believed in the dream, but it had all been a lie. Summer was the ultimate liar. And even if it weren't for that calamity, even if she were the lovely illusion he'd believed in, he couldn't live with the press pouncing on them every time one of them had so much as a conversation with another attractive person. He didn't want his marriage to be a feast for public consumption. He wanted a real marriage—a private, personal bonding of two souls—not some mirage of perfect love that would heighten Summer's popularity.

"I don't need this," he growled as he stood up.

"Sit back down," Viola commanded in her bossy way.

Strange that, in his hopeless mood, he found her firm manner oddly comforting.

Slowly, he sank back into the chair, Summer's favorite chair, which happened to be his favorite, too.

"I may be a pushy old lady, who doesn't know half as much as she should, but I know you two belong together."

"Not anymore. Too many things have happened. The past…our first baby…all the lies. I don't want everything we do to be magnified by the media."

"Summer is a wonderful girl, and you know it! Thurman was a real stinker. Hasn't he cost us all enough? As for the press—why do you care so much about what other people think?"

"It's not that simple."

"I say it is. I say maybe you're too proud, too arrogant. And maybe, despite your bluster, you're something of a coward."

He scowled at her.

"I know this because I've been guilty of the same thing at times. When anything bad is written about Summer, my friends all tease me. I don't like it. I feel put down and ashamed. But they're jealous, you see, of her success. Not that any of them will admit it. But don't they just love it when unkind words are written about Summer or an unflattering picture of her is taken? I fall for their bluster every time and blame Summer. Either she sets me straight or I get my bearings back on my own. All the negative stuff is backward praise in a way. People see how wonderful she is and want a part of her. It's up to me to stay centered and put her first and everybody else last—where they belong."

"We've got an ugly past to live down, as well."

"When you've lived as long as I have, you learn you can live anything down."

"Look, our lifestyles just aren't compatible."

"Then modify them. Maybe it won't take as much give on your part as you think. When two people who are right for each other come together, the most insurmountable obstacles can be conquered."

"I've gotta go."

"My, but you're stubborn. It's probably one of the reasons you're so successful. You stick to what you decide to do, and do it. But in this case, you're wrong. You're making the biggest mistake of your life."

"Usually, I go with my gut. This time, though, I made an intelligent decision, based on past and present experience—that's all."

"Maybe you should stick with your gut."

"Not smart. She's too good of an actress. She throws off my instincts."

"Has this all been about revenge, then—about you wanting to get even with her for what happened fifteen years ago?"

"Hell, no."

"Well, too bad, 'cause you'd sure be even with her if it was. You really hurt her this time. I haven't seen her like this since she failed to carry your first child. It seems so unfair that here she is pregnant again, you both have a glorious second chance, but you're walking out on her like before. You just about killed her last time."

"I don't need this."

"I say you do. When you were in jail, Thurman found out she was pregnant and sent her away to New Orleans to have your baby. He didn't want you or anybody else to know about the baby because he was afraid it might sway public opinion in your favor. There were people, even back then, who sided with you and didn't like the way Thurman was using his pull to rush the due process of law.

"Did you know Summer tried to contact you shortly before she miscarried?"

"You're not telling me anything I don't already know."

Viola ignored his protest. "Summer was inconsolable when she couldn't find you. Finally, she felt that she had nowhere to go but back to New Orleans, and that's where she lost the baby. Summer had the saddest little funeral for that child. Not that I could go. I was too busy tending to my dying daughter. When Summer finally came home to stay, she was different, changed.

"Then Anna, her mother, died. Summer blamed Thurman for everything that had happened, for the end of her mother's remission, for losing you, for the death of the baby. She said she couldn't live in this town with her memories, so she broke away from all of us and went to New York. That's where she took bit parts while going to college in her spare time. I sent money. She worked herself to the bone in an effort to forget you. But she never could."

"I had my own problems back then."

The ancients and the wise say a man can learn the greatest truths of the universe in an instant. Suddenly, that was true for Zach. No sooner had he said those bitter words than his perspective shifted dramatically. All the pieces of the story he had imagined to be the truth about his love affair with Summer arranged themselves in a new and different order with a new and different meaning.

Had he been hurt and too bitter to consider what Summer had gone through? He had. And he hadn't known the half of it. When she'd sought him out in Houston, how coldly he'd rejected her.

*Just as he was rejecting her now.*

All that had ever mattered was their love for each other. If they'd kept their focus on that, no one could have touched them.

The pain he felt was staggering. He'd hurt Summer terribly, more than Thurman ever had. Because he'd been stubbornly focused on his own grievances. And blind to hers.

The image of that single tear trickling down her beautiful face tugged at his heart. Why hadn't he listened to his instinct and drawn her close and kissed her tears away?

"I've said my piece, so you can go now," Viola said as she laid a gnarled hand on Silas, who purred in her lap.

For a long moment, Zach sat where he was, stunned. Without Summer beside him, he faced nothing but long years of emptiness. He would fill up his days with work, but the nights would be long and lonely. There would be no one to hold him in the darkness. No one to care about his failures or share his successes. He would be forever diminished without her love.

And he was throwing it all away.

"You have a plane to catch, don't you?"

"Thank you for the cookies and tea," he muttered mechanically, like someone in a dream.

He stared at the spot on the porch where he'd kissed Summer as a girl. She'd been so blushingly shy and lovely. When he'd kissed the woman in that same spot fifteen years later, she'd been hurt and defiant and in denial, but he'd seen into her heart and had fallen in love with her all over again.

He loved her.

He wasn't going to stop loving her just because he willed himself to do so. His love for her was the truest and strongest part of him. By sending her and his child away, he faced the death of everything that would ever matter to him.

He had to make this right.

He needed Summer and their child.

Damn the press. Why hadn't he seen that he should put her first, instead of his own damn ego? She'd carried his child and lost it while her mother had been gravely ill. The thought of her alone and pregnant again was excruciatingly unbearable. If anything happened to her or the baby because of his horrible cruelty, he would never forgive himself.

He had to take care of them. He had to find a way to protect them from the press instead of blaming Summer for the made-up headlines. And when he couldn't protect them, he'd endure the media coverage…. If only Summer would forgive him and take him back.

# Thirteen

It was raining outside the theater, pouring. Not that Summer cared.

Opening nights were all about families and friends. Thus, her dressing room and bathroom overflowed with vivid bouquets of flowers, embossed cards from the greats and the near-greats and telegrams, as well. Everybody she remotely cared about was packed inside these two tiny rooms with her. Everybody except Zach, the one person who mattered most.

As she waited for her place to be called, her grandmother and brother sat to her left on her long couch, while her dresser, hairdresser and agent sat to the right. It was a tight squeeze, but Summer needed their support desperately because Zach wasn't here.

She still felt raw and shaken from their breakup, and she'd kept people with her constantly so she wouldn't break down when the press asked their prying questions.

She kept telling herself she needed to accept that he was

gone so she could move on from this profound pain, but some part of her refused to believe he was out of her life forever. She kept hoping against hope for a miracle. He would relent and forgive her…. And love her. She wanted this miracle more than ever, and not solely because she was carrying his child.

That's why she was barely listening to the buzz around her, why she couldn't stop staring past Gram toward the door, why she couldn't stop hoping the door would open and she'd find him standing there. If only he'd walk in, take her in his arms and say everything was all right.

Then, only then, would she be whole and happy again. She didn't want to get over him. She simply wanted him in her life, in her baby's life, every day for the rest of her days. She wanted to wake up to his face on the pillow and go to sleep with the same vision, and she couldn't seem to get past that heartfelt desire. So for days—or was it weeks, she'd lost count—she'd lingered in a dreadful suspended state of suffering.

She was an actress, so she hid her pain with brilliant smiles and quick laughter, but those who knew her weren't fooled.

Suddenly, there was a roar in her ears, and she felt faint.

Summer closed her eyes and wished them all gone. She needed some alone time before the places were called to get her mind off Zach and onto her character, but everybody else was drinking champagne and having way too good a time to leave the couches.

Suddenly Paolo stormed into the dressing room. His expression was so serious when he yelled for everybody to be quiet that the uproar died instantly. He motioned for them all to leave, and because of his imperious manner, Paolo got what he wanted. They fled.

Normally, she would have thought his actions meant her reviews were bad and he'd come to tell her this bitter truth, but tonight she couldn't stop thinking about Zach long enough to care.

Paolo took her hand, squeezed it fiercely. "*Bella!* I came to tell you your reviews are sensational! The critics loved you in the previews! They adore you! We've got a hit!"

"You're sure?"

"I'm sure."

"Oh."

"Is that all you can say?" he thundered, quite put out at her lack of enthusiasm.

"I'm thrilled. Of course, I'm thrilled," she whispered dully as the overture began and places were called.

She was hardly aware of the music or of Paolo as she rose.

Paolo kissed her cheek and shoved her toward the door. "Go out there and break a leg."

She was on her way out the door when she remembered her secret ritual on opening nights. Walking swiftly to her dressing table, she flung open a drawer and removed the white-leather volume with fading gilt letters on its covers. She opened it and pressed her lips gently against the withered, yellowed rose.

Then she replaced the cherished volume and ran.

Lightning lit the sky. Thunder reverberated almost instantly.

Then all was dark again as torrents of rain slashed the jet.

Inside, Zach jammed his cell phone into his pocket impatiently and began to pace the length of the plane. He should have been in Manhattan hours ago, before Summer's play even started. He'd taken a box seat. He'd planned to be in it when she came onstage. He'd never make curtain call now.

He went to the liquor cabinet and grabbed a bottle of scotch. Splashing it into a glass, he drank deeply. Then he fumbled in his other pocket to make sure the tiny, black-velvet box was still there. He'd told himself to get rid of the ring, but he hadn't. Had he known even then that he couldn't live without her?

Pulling the ring out, he lifted the lid. The enormous engagement diamond shot sparks at him as he imagined himself slipping it onto her beautiful hand. If only, she'd have him after he'd pushed her away.

He hated this feeling of being in limbo, on edge, vulnerable. Only his need for her could reduce him to this.

What if Summer said no?

"Stop!" Zach said when he saw Summer's name blazing in red neon atop a brightly lit marquee.

Grabbing the dozens of red roses he'd bought her, he got out of the limo in the middle of traffic and made a dash across the street for the theater.

Brakes squealed. Horns honked. Cabbies cursed him. A reporter yelled his name and took his picture. But he didn't care.

Maybe he could still catch her grand finale.

When he opened the doors of the theater, he heard the roar of applause and a thousand bravos.

They loved her!

His heart swelled with joy and admiration. He loved her, too, and he was nearly bursting with pride at all she'd accomplished. No wonder so many people craved the details of her life. They saw her as a princess in a fairy tale, and they wanted a place in the dream.

He remembered when she'd wowed everybody in Bonne Terre in her high-school production of *Grease*. Zach had believed in her dream then. He had wanted her to succeed, and now she had.

He was running down the center aisle of the orchestra section when she walked onto the stage in a glittering gold gown to take her final curtain call. At the sight of her, so slim and stunningly lovely, the crowd went even wilder, yelling her name along with more bravos.

There must have been two thousand people in that theater, and they were packed to the rafters.

She bowed gracefully as people stood cheering.

Zach waved and called her name, but she couldn't hear him over the roar of her audience.

Everyone began to throw roses at the stage.

This was her moment. He stopped and waited, allowing her to shine.

There would be time later to take her in his arms, to tell her how sorry he was he'd hurt her, to swear to her he'd never do it again, to beg for her forgiveness. He'd tell her he wanted to marry her so he could spend the rest of his life making it up to her.

The past didn't matter. Her fame didn't matter. Only she and their baby and the life they would make together was important to him.

Blinded by the stage lights and feeling a little faint, Summer took another deep bow. When she straightened, she raised her hands and blew kisses as the audience continued to clap.

They stomped and screamed louder, so she bowed a final time.

This time when she straightened she heard a man on stage right call her name.

*His* voice shuddered through her, or did she only imagine him there?

Hoping, she turned and was overjoyed to see a tall man in a dark suit holding the biggest bouquet of roses she'd ever seen.

"Zach," she whispered, not really believing what she saw, as she took a faltering step toward him. She sucked in a breath. "Is it really you? Or am I dreaming? Oh, please, God, don't let me be dreaming!"

Then he came nearer, and his dear face with all those hard angles came into focus, and she saw that his eyes were warm and filled with love. He smiled sheepishly, but he dazzled her just the same.

"Oh, Zach. You came. You really came. I wanted you here so much. You'll never know…how much."

Handing her the huge bouquet of red roses, he swept her into his arms and kissed her.

Dozens of flashes exploded. The crowd roared, loving him, loving her, loving them together because their fairy tale had come true.

She couldn't believe he'd come tonight, that maybe he still loved her. But then she could believe it because his kisses took her breath away as did the tears shining in his beautiful, dark eyes.

"Forgive me," he whispered. "Love me…. Please love me again or I'll die."

"Oh, Zach…. With all my heart," she replied. "Always. And forever."


Although the corridor outside Summer's dressing room was noisy, Summer was aware of nothing except Zach, who was on bended knee, looking up at her, his expression fierce, almost desperate, as he clutched her hand.

"Tell me you weren't playing a part for the crowd when you promised to love me out there, sweetheart."

"I wasn't."

"I wouldn't blame you if you were. I deserve that…and worse."

"I've loved you since I was thirteen. I never stopped loving you. I never will."

"I never stopped loving you, either. I'm sorry I was so brutal when you came to Louisiana to tell me about our baby. You were so beautiful in pink, so damned beautiful, so sad…."

And I deliberately hurt you. Maybe because I felt so much and was determined to ignore those feelings. Gram called me a fool for not listening to my gut and a coward for pushing you and your love away, and she was right."

"It's okay. It's okay." Gently Summer cupped his rugged face in her hands. "It's okay. I understand. I do."

"To ever think you weren't worth whatever it costs to make our life together was the second biggest mistake of my life. The first was that I should have stood by you fifteen years ago instead of blaming you for not standing by me. I've always been a selfish, egotistical bastard."

"I should have done better by you, too."

"We can't go back," he said. "Or control the events of the past. We can only control how we view them."

"And the press? You really think you'll be able to stand all the fuss?"

"I don't care what the world thinks about me or you. Whatever we have together is true. It is the strongest force in my life…. Stronger even than my ambition, stronger than any lie the vicious press can write or say. I haven't given a damn about work since we've been apart. Nothing matters to me as much as you and our child. Nothing. I can't change the past, but together we can change our future."

She'd waited so long to hear such words from him, to feel loved by him so completely. Happiness overflowed in her heart.

"Will you marry me, then, Summer Wallace? Will you honor me by becoming Mrs. Zach Torr?"

"What? And give up my stage name?" she teased.

He pulled a black-velvet box out of his hand and opened it. The diamond sparkled with a vengeance.

But her eyes shone even brighter as she stared down at him. "Oh, my! You could persuade a lot of girls with a rock that size."

"You're the only one I want, and you didn't answer the question."

"That's because I'm still in shock. But, yes. Yes!" she cried as he slid the ring onto her finger. "Yes!"

"Then kiss me, Summer. This time I won't complain about an Oscar performance."

She laughed as she pulled his face up to hers and pressed her lips to his and did just as he commanded, for a very long time. Only it wasn't a performance, it was true and real.

She'd always been true and real. He would never doubt her again.

"Mrs. Zach Torr," she breathed in an awed tone when he finally released her.

A single tear traced down her cheek. Only this time it was a tear of joy.


Summer had never had more fun at a cast party than she was having tonight with Zach beside her and his ring glimmering on her left hand. At the same time she couldn't wait to steal away from the lavish affair, so she could spend the rest of the night with her fiancé.

But they had forever, didn't they? Or at least as long as they both should live.

Because they'd known the reviews would be good, the producers were out to impress. They'd rented a fabulous ballroom at the top of one of New York's most prestigious hotels. The food was excellent; the champagne vintage. She had to stay awhile because she was the star.

When Hugh crashed the party unexpectedly and began garnering more press than anybody else, she tensed, whispering to Zach that she'd tell the show's producers to make him leave.

Zach pressed a fingertip to her lips. "Let him stay, sweetheart. I don't care. The press can write whatever they want about the three of us."

"You really don't care?"

"I swear it. Don't worry about me. Introduce me to the bastard. I'll even pose with him. Go do what you have to do. Work the crowd. Let the photographers take the appropriate pictures of you with your cast and producers. Because the sooner you do, the sooner we can leave and have the rest of the night for each other."

She listened to his sure, calm voice, which didn't hold the faintest trace of jealousy, and felt as if she'd come home. At last.

Happiness filled her. So much happiness, she couldn't speak.

"Oh, Zach."

He pulled her into his arms. For a long moment, as he held her close, she realized that this was her new life, their shared life. He was part of all she was, just as she would be part of all he was. No more scandals stood between them.

They would be together forever.

# Epilogue

The stairs creaked as Summer carried Terri, who was bundled in pink blankets and asleep, up to the nursery. But she couldn't put her beautiful, dark-haired little girl in the crib. The baby was too soft and warm and cuddly, and every minute Summer held her was too precious.

The joy-filled days passed so fast. Summer had given herself a year off for maternity leave, and already four months of it were gone. So she sat in the rocker and began to sing to her little girl while she stared out at the pines that fringed the house that had belonged to her family for more than a hundred years.

Summer loved the time she and Zach spent in this old house, the time when they left their nannies and servants in their larger residences in Houston and New York, and they could be together with Gram and Tuck.

Downstairs Gram was cooking a dinner for all of them, so the house was fragrant with the rich aroma of Cajun spices.

Nick had supplied Gram with shrimp, and she'd promised them all, including Nick, a big pot of gumbo.

Nick, who adored Terri so much he'd even made a place in his heart for Summer, would be joining them.

Summer heard Zach's Mercedes in the drive. Then the screen door banged behind him. Would that man ever learn to shut a door quietly when it was nap time?

"Summer!" Zach hollered.

"Up here," she called down to him softly and was relieved when he didn't yell again. Much as she adored Terri, like any other new mother, she counted on having a breather when her little darling snoozed.

Zach strode silently into the room and knelt beside them. Reaching out his hand he touched Terri's cheek. In her sleep, the baby smiled. Then she grabbed on to his little finger, and he gasped.

The baby's pale fingers with their little fingernails were so tiny and perfect; his tanned ones so large and blunt.

"Can I hold her?" he whispered.

Summer nodded, lifting their daughter into his arms. She got up so he could have the rocker.

"She's got me. I'm afraid I'll never be able to be stern and say no to her," he whispered. "I'll spoil her rotten."

"Well, we won't have to discipline her for a while."

Summer's eyes pooled with tears of happiness as she watched her two raven-haired darlings—her rugged husband and their trusting and innocent baby daughter.

She wished she could hold on to this moment.

The past would always be a part of them, especially the loss of their first daughter. But love filled Summer's days now with all its richly rewarding experiences. Marriage. Motherhood.

Life was so wonderful, she was determined to savor every sparkling moment of her shared happiness with Zach.

"Come here," he whispered as he got up to put their baby in her crib.

Turning to Summer, he took her in his arms and pressed her tightly against him.

"I love you," he said.

He told her that every day, and she never tired of hearing it.

She was glad that love was no longer a four-letter word he equated with hell. She was glad their love had become the guiding force in his life.

As it was in hers.

* * * * *

# REQUEST YOUR FREE BOOKS!

## 2 FREE NOVELS PLUS 2 FREE GIFTS!

**◈ Harlequin®**

## *Desire*

### ALWAYS POWERFUL, PASSIONATE AND PROVOCATIVE

**YES!** Please send me 2 FREE Harlequin Desire® novels and my 2 FREE gifts (gifts are worth about $10). After receiving them, if I don't wish to receive any more books, I can return the shipping statement marked "cancel." If I don't cancel, I will receive 6 brand-new novels every month and be billed just $4.30 per book in the U.S. or $4.99 per book in Canada. That's a saving of at least 14% off the cover price! It's quite a bargain! Shipping and handling is just 50¢ per book in the U.S. and 75¢ per book in Canada.* I understand that accepting the 2 free books and gifts places me under no obligation to buy anything. I can always return a shipment and cancel at any time. Even if I never buy another book, the two free books and gifts are mine to keep forever.

225/326 HDN FEF3

| | |
|---|---|
| Name | (PLEASE PRINT) |

| | |
|---|---|
| Address | Apt. # |

| | | |
|---|---|---|
| City | State/Prov. | Zip/Postal Code |

Signature (if under 18, a parent or guardian must sign)

### Mail to the **Reader Service:**

**IN U.S.A.:** P.O. Box 1867, Buffalo, NY 14240-1867
**IN CANADA:** P.O. Box 609, Fort Erie, Ontario L2A 5X3

Not valid for current subscribers to Harlequin Desire books.

**Want to try two free books from another line?**
**Call 1-800-873-8635 or visit www.ReaderService.com.**

* Terms and prices subject to change without notice. Prices do not include applicable taxes. Sales tax applicable in N.Y. Canadian residents will be charged applicable taxes. Offer not valid in Quebec. This offer is limited to one order per household. All orders subject to credit approval. Credit or debit balances in a customer's account(s) may be offset by any other outstanding balance owed by or to the customer. Please allow 4 to 6 weeks for delivery. Offer available while quantities last.

**Your Privacy**—The Reader Service is committed to protecting your privacy. Our Privacy Policy is available online at www.ReaderService.com or upon request from the Reader Service.

We make a portion of our mailing list available to reputable third parties that offer products we believe may interest you. If you prefer that we not exchange your name with third parties, or if you wish to clarify or modify your communication preferences, please visit us at www.ReaderService.com/consumerchoice or write to us at Reader Service Preference Service, P.O. Box 9062, Buffalo, NY 14269. Include your complete name and address.

HDES11B